A THIRD MOMENT IN TIME

A Collection of Short Stories

SUSAN STOKER

THE BULLY

by Susan Stoker

ABOUT THE BOOK

Annie Fletcher has an idyllic life. A step-father who loves her. Siblings who mean the world to her. And a whole slew of overprotective "uncles" who are always there for her.

But when a bully at school targets the seventh-grader, Annie's on her own. But after getting some advice from Truck…it's game on.

**This story was originally included in the Naughty & Nice Aces Press holiday anthology which came out in December of 2021 and is no longer available.

THE BULLY

EMILY GLANCED toward the front door when she heard it open. She waited to see her daughter's happy face as she entered the house after school. It was hard to believe Annie was twelve, and already in the seventh grade. She'd always be her little baby, but she was growing up fast.

But instead of Annie coming into the kitchen, pulling herself up on one of the chairs at the table and chattering happily about what happened in school that day, she clomped right past the doorway and headed for her room without a word.

"Annie?" Emily called out.

In response, she heard her daughter's bedroom door slam shut.

Blinking in surprise, Emily stood in the middle of the kitchen, frowning in the direction of the hallway where Annie had disappeared. Deciding to give her some time, Emily turned back to the lasagna sauce she was putting together for dinner. Fletch should be home from the base in an hour and she needed to get the pasta in the oven if it was going to be ready by the time he arrived.

Ethan, their son, was two and currently occupied by a video on the TV. Emily was doubly concerned about Annie because one of her favorite things in the world was her little brother. She doted on Ethan. Ever since he was born, Annie was like a second mother to him.

Emily remembered when they'd first realized the depth of Annie's love for her brother. Ethan was around four months old, and Annie had begun to eat much less at dinner. It took her and Fletch a couple weeks to figure out what was going on. Annie thought her brother wasn't getting enough to eat, so she was hiding food and bringing it to him at night, after everyone went to sleep.

Apparently, she remembered how Emily would forego food so Annie herself could eat, and was attempting to do the same for her brother.

Fletch had a long talk with her, explaining that they had plenty of money to buy food for all of them and, as Ethan was a baby, he could only eat formula.

Annie constantly looked after her brother, even

after that. Another time, while doing yardwork, Fletch found around a hundred of Annie's little plastic Army men on the ground outside Ethan's window. When he asked her about it, she told him they were there to protect Ethan from anyone trying to break into his room.

She also had a tendency to climb into his bed in the middle of the night. Even now, when Emily or Fletch went into Ethan's room in the morning, they'd sometimes find their daughter sleeping curled around her brother. She read to him regularly. Would sit with him for hours, reading the same book over and over again and never seeming to get tired of it.

So the fact that Annie came into the house and completely ignored her baby brother said more about her mood than anything else could.

After putting the lasagna into the oven, Emily washed her hands and, making sure Ethan was still occupied, headed for Annie's room. She lightly tapped on the door.

"Annie?"

"Go away!" her daughter said, her voice sounding muffled.

Emily frowned. "I'm making lasagna for dinner," she told her daughter, knowing how much Annie loved the dish.

"I'm not hungry!" was her response.

"You want to talk about what's bothering you?" Emily asked. "I'm a good listener."

"No! I just want to be alone!"

She sighed and backed away from the door. Annie was usually a very happy-go-lucky kid. Not much got her down. Emily had been warned about the pre-teen years, and about seventh grade girls especially, but she'd hoped, Annie being the tomboy that she was, she might avoid some of the turbulent emotions that came with being a teenager. It seemed that wasn't the case.

Emily spent the next hour hoping Annie would come out of her room and go back to being her normal happy self, but that didn't happen. She sent a text to Mary, knowing how close her daughter was to the other woman, and asked if she and Truck might want to come over for dinner.

Luckily, Mary agreed immediately, making Emily sigh in relief. All her friends were awesome. They never hesitated to babysit when she wanted some alone time with her husband, and she did the same for them. Rayne and Ghost had just had their first child, a boy they'd named Billy. Kassie and Hollywood's daughter, Kate, was a year younger than Ethan, and watching the two toddlers play together was adorable and heartwarming.

Their husbands were a big help with the kids as

well, now more than ever. They were all transitioning to administrative roles within the Delta Force organization, and Emily couldn't say she was upset about it. Fletch loved serving his country, but Emily, and the rest of her friends, worried obsessively about them when they were deployed on dangerous missions.

By the time Fletch arrived home, Emily still hadn't seen her daughter, and she was a nervous wreck. This wasn't her Annie at all, and Emily hated that her daughter wouldn't talk to her. For the first six or so years of her life, they'd only had each other. They were best friends. Even after meeting Fletch, who her daughter completely adored, the bond between her and Annie remained strong. So her daughter not speaking to her felt incredibly wrong to Emily.

"What's wrong?" Fletch asked the second he saw his wife.

Emily wasn't surprised he could tell something was up.

He gathered her close, wrapping one arm around her waist and palming her cheek. "Ethan okay?" he asked.

Emily nodded. "Yeah. It's Annie."

"Annie?" Fletch asked in surprise. "What's wrong with her?"

"I don't know, she won't talk to me. She came

home from school in an awful mood. Went straight to her room without even greeting Ethan."

Fletch frowned. He also knew how much her brother meant to her. "Is that why you invited Mary and Truck over for dinner?" he asked.

Emily couldn't help but smile. Mary had probably texted Truck, who'd most likely asked Fletch what time they should come over. "Yeah. She's always been close to them. I figure if she won't talk to me, maybe she'll tell one of them what's bothering her."

"I'm not ready," Fletch sighed.

Emily frowned in confusion. "For what?" she asked.

"For Annie to grow up. I want her to be my sprite forever."

"She will," Emily reassured him.

Fletch shook his head. "No. She already doesn't look to me for everything anymore, which I hate. I'm no longer Daddy Fletch, I'm 'Dad.' She's gonna go to high school, and her friends are going to be more important than spending time with us. It won't be cool to hang out with her dad, crawling all over the tanks at the motor pool on base. She's gonna marry Frankie, move away, and we'll have to beg her to come home every now and then to see us."

Emily couldn't help but laugh. "You're being as dramatic as our pre-teen," she scolded.

"I know," Fletch said morosely. "I just love her so much and hate to think of the day she'll leave to go to college. I have no doubt she's going to do amazing things, but still…" His voice trailed off.

"How about we get through one crisis at a time before we think about her moving out and getting married?" Emily suggested.

"Have I told you today how much I love you?" Fletch asked.

Emily smiled up at him. "Today? Yes. This morning before you left for work. But this afternoon? No."

"I love you," Fletch said immediately. "So much it's almost scary."

Emily beamed. "I love you too."

"I want another baby."

Emily blinked in surprise. "What? Like, right this second?"

Fletch chuckled. "Not sure that's possible, but eventually, yes. At least one more. Maybe two."

Ethan was an easy baby, but Emily wasn't sure she was ready for another just yet. Though she couldn't deny she wanted more children. "I want that too. I'm thinking spacing them out is a good thing though. Let's get Ethan potty trained, in preschool, then we'll talk about having another."

"Four years apart," Fletch said with a nod. "That

sounds good. We can get one graduated from high school before the next starts. They won't be in each other's shadow. And you won't have too many babies in the house at the same time."

Emily loved this man so much. Even when they were planning their family, his first thought was about her.

"But no more girls," he said sternly. "Boys."

Emily rolled her eyes. "It's your sperm that decides, not my reproductive organs," she told him.

Fletch nodded. "Boys it is then," he said decisively.

Emily shook her head in exasperation. She couldn't deny that boys were easier in some ways, but she couldn't help but think about how amazing Fletch was with Annie. He was protective—overprotective, at times—but understanding and gentle. He also had no problem letting Annie be herself. If she wanted to play in the dirt, he let her. If she wanted to wear pants instead of a dress, he didn't push. Anything his Annie wanted, she got.

"So, Ethan's two. If we want four years between them, that gives us a little over a year before we start trying to get pregnant again. So you should probably go off birth control in thirteen months or so."

Emily chuckled. "You've got it all figured out, huh?" she asked. She couldn't help but squirm in his hold, thinking about the act of making their future babies. When Fletch got it in his head to do something, he was one hundred percent committed. Before Ethan was conceived, her husband was insatiable in the bedroom. Doing everything in his power to knock her up.

"Yup," he said with a gleam in his eye.

"I'm thinking we're gonna need to practice a lot," Emily teased. "I mean, we wouldn't want to mess up your plans and all."

Fletch's eyes dilated, and he moved his other hand to her face, tilting it up toward him. "I love seeing you pregnant," he told her. "You seriously glow. And knowing I did that, that our love made a baby...it's amazing. Not to mention, the knocking-you-up part is pretty damn exciting. Every time I come inside you, I can't help but think about you getting pregnant. It's...I can't describe how it feels. Knowing our love might create another child for us to cherish. You're *my* miracle, Miracle Emily Grant Fletcher, and I'll do everything in my power to show you each and every day how much I love you."

"You already do," Emily whispered. How she'd ended up with this man, she'd never know. She thought back to when they met, when she was desperate for a cheap place to live, everything that happened with the man who was blackmailing her, and how scared she'd been. As soon as Fletch found out what was going on, he sprang into action. Making sure she and Annie were safe. He'd proven time and time again that he'd do whatever it took to give her a safe and happy life. Even through the bumps in the road, she'd always been able to count on him.

Fletch's head dropped and he kissed her. It wasn't a chaste kiss either. He took her lips with a passion usually reserved for their bedroom. He still held her face, and Emily grabbed hold of his waist with both hands to keep herself upright. But Fletch wouldn't let her fall. No way. He was her rock.

The sound of the doorbell surprised Emily, and she jerked in Fletch's arms.

"Damn Truck and his shit timing," Fletch grumbled, as he pulled away from her.

She couldn't help but smile. Spontaneous sex was never something they'd had the luxury of indulging in. Not with Annie around. And now with two children, their lovemaking was confined to their bedroom, after their kids were fast asleep.

But the anticipation of making love to her husband was always enough to keep Emily on edge until they were finally alone. It somehow made sex even better.

"Tonight," he whispered before kissing her forehead. "After Truck and Mary straighten Annie out, after our daughter is back to her smiley self, after we get Ethan put down, fat and happy in his crib, I'm gonna practice that baby-making. Gotta make sure I'm ready for the real thing in a few months."

Emily simply shook her head. Fletch didn't need to practice anything. He was already an expert at the whole baby-making thing. It was fortunate she lived now, and not in a time when there wasn't birth control. She had a feeling she'd end up having a baby a year otherwise.

"Go let our friends in," she told him with a shake of her head.

"You want to serve dinner before or after they talk to Annie?" Fletch asked.

"After," Emily said without hesitation. "The last thing I want is a sulky daughter at the dinner table."

"Good point." Fletch leaned down, kissed her once more. A hard and fast kiss, before brushing his thumb over her cheek and turning to let Mary and Truck in.

Emily watched him go and sighed in contentment. Fletch was awesome, and she'd never get tired of having him look after her and their children.

She headed into the living room and picked up Ethan. He complained a bit, until he heard voices coming from the front of the house. Her son loved guests, probably because he got a ton of attention, which was his second favorite thing. The first being his sister.

Mary and Truck entered the living room, and Mary made a beeline for Ethan. Emily grinned as she held him out to her friend. Ethan babbled happily as Mary bounced him on her hip.

"Hi," Emily said. "Thanks for coming over."

"Of course. I was just sitting there wondering what I was going to make for dinner when you texted. No one tells you when you're little that you'll spend half your life attempting to decide what to have for dinner. It sucks. So not having to make that decision for one night is heaven."

Emily laughed. Mary wasn't wrong. She didn't have the heart to tell her it only got worse once you had kids. Because then, whatever you decided to have for dinner, someone inevitably turned up their nose and didn't want to eat it. Truck and Mary were in the process of trying to adopt a pair of siblings from India. She figured it would be even tougher for her friend to come up with menus, considering their future kids would come from a different culture. But she said none of that, simply grateful they were here to try to coax Annie out of her doldrums.

"She in her room?" Truck asked.

Emily nodded.

"I'll go talk to her," the large man said. To many,

Truck could be intimidating. He was a freaking giant of a man. Tall and muscular. And he had a gnarly scar on his cheek. But to Emily, and Annie, he was just Truck. A teddy bear who would never hurt them.

"Thank you," Emily said quietly.

"You don't have to thank me for coming to see Annie," Truck said quietly. "I love her like she's my own. I'd do anything for her. *Anything*." And with that, he turned and headed for the hallway that led to her room.

"Damn," Mary mumbled, wiping her cheek with her shoulder. "I can't believe I held out so long on following through with this adoption. Truck's going to make an amazing father."

"Yes, he is," Emily agreed. "Come on, I'm thinking we both need a large glass of wine. Annie's not even a teenager yet. I'm not sure I'm going to survive."

"You will," Mary said. "Because she's a good kid. Whatever's bothering her is probably more about someone else than her. Truck'll figure it out and she'll be back to be our Annie. Maybe I'll challenge her to a spin around the track on her tank after dinner."

Emily chuckled. "You'll lose," she warned. "She's become even more competitive as she's gotten older. And no one beats her on her own track in her own backyard."

"I know," Mary said, unconcerned. "I just like to challenge her. If she's serious about wanting to be a special forces solder like her dad, she's gonna need to be better than good. She's gonna need to have a thick skin and a hunger inside her to be the best she can be, regardless of what anyone else tells her. I'm ready to talk smack with her, piss her off, and show her that it doesn't matter what others say, it matters what she wants deep inside."

Emily sniffed. That, right there, was one of a million reasons why she loved her friends. They all knew Annie wanted to be special forces, and they also knew how hard that goal was, especially in today's military. But no one would tell Annie she couldn't do it. They'd encourage her every step of the way.

"Come on," Emily said, taking a deep breath. "If Fletch sees me crying, he'll want to know why and I don't want him mad at you."

"Whatever," Mary said with a roll of her eyes. "I'm not scared of your husband."

Emily grinned. "No, but he could steal Ethan from you and not let you hold him the rest of the night," she teased.

"He wouldn't dare," Mary growled, holding Ethan closer.

Emily burst out laughing. "Let's go. I can hear the

wine calling our names. I hope Truck can get Annie to open up in the meantime."

"He will," Mary said confidently.

———

Annie sat in her closet with her back against the wall. Her dad had helped her make this space in the closet in their new house, when they'd moved in. She'd wanted a "bunker" like he'd talked about having to lie in when he was deployed. She thought it would be cool to have a fort inside her room, where she could pretend to be a soldier just like her dad and his friends.

For as long as she could remember, she'd wanted to be a soldier. She wanted to keep people safe and rescue them from the bad guys. She could remember watching *Wonder Woman* on TV with her mom, before they met Fletch. The one with the lady with the tiny waist and beautiful long brown hair. The show was old, and kind of cheesy, but Annie had still been fascinated with the concept. She would play by herself for hours after watching an episode. First, she'd be Wonder Woman, spinning in circles and pretending to save people from bad guys. Then she'd switch it up, and be the one who needed saving.

Then she'd met Fletch and his friends...who were

real live heroes, just like Wonder Woman. They went to other countries and hunkered down in foxholes, spying on the bad guys until they discovered their weaknesses, then they'd spring out of the hole and save the day.

Of course, Annie had no idea what her dad *really* did when he was deployed. He never said, and she knew better than to ask. But after being rescued by her dad and his team in real life, Annie adored them even more, and her determination to be just like them grew by leaps and bounds.

Though there were some days, like today, when everything she'd ever dreamed about doing with her life felt stupid. *She* felt stupid.

Annie hated that Carrie, a popular girl from school who'd been a bully for a long as Annie had known her, could make her feel so bad about herself.

A knock on her door sounded, and Annie yelled, "I'm not hungry!" without even waiting to hear what her mom said. It had to be dinnertime, but Annie was in no mood to eat.

"Hey, sprite," a deep voice said, as Truck poked his head into her room. "Can I come in?"

Annie's heart leaped with joy. Truck was here! She loved all her dad's friend, but she had a special place in her heart for this man. Then she remembered she was in a bad mood. "Whatever," she mumbled.

She was glad when Truck ignored her less-than-welcoming response and came in. He shut the door behind him and walked over to the open closet door. He sat down, then fell backward and stared up at the ceiling. "I heard you had a bad day."

Annie sighed. Why couldn't everyone just leave her alone? Although she had to admit it was easier to talk to Truck when he wasn't looking at her. He was staring up at the ceiling as if it was the most interesting thing he'd ever seen in his life. Annie couldn't see it from where she was at the back of the closet, but unless someone had come in here while she was at school and painted stars on it or something, it was just a plain white ceiling.

"I hate school," she told Truck forcefully. "It's stupid."

"Is this about that bully who keeps bothering you?" Truck asked.

Annie shouldn't have been surprised he remembered. Other than that time he'd had amnesia and forgot everything that had happened recently in his life, he seemed to remember every single word she said.

She sighed. "Why are people so mean?"

Truck turned over and propped his head on his hand. "I don't know. I guess ignoring the bully isn't working?" he asked.

Annie shrugged. "I don't care what she says about me. She's a jerk. All she cares about is making sure her hair is perfect, and you should see how much makeup she wears. It's gross. She's always going after the boys and giggling whenever they say anything. It's stupid."

"Did she say something to you today?" Truck asked.

Annie looked down at her hands. "She always says shit to me," she told him. Then she brought her head up and met his gaze. "I've gotten used to ignoring her. But today, she started in on the new boy in our class. He goes to special classes, but he eats lunch the same time we do. The only person who ever sits with him is his aide, and she wasn't there today. He looked lonely, so Amy and I went to his table to eat.

"Stupid Carrie came over with her two best friends and they started calling him a retard and being especially mean. I told her to go away, and that's when she started saying all sorts of stuff about Frankie. I mean, she doesn't even *know* him, so why would she feel as if it's okay to make fun of him?"

"What'd she say?" Truck asked.

Annie sighed. "Just the usual stuff. That it was obvious I liked retarded guys since I was dating one, and now I was eating lunch with one. She wanted to know if Frankie knew I was cheating on him with

Robert. Then she laughed and said something about me being a virgin for the rest of my life because no one would dare come anywhere near me, since I'm such a tomboy and like rolling around in the dirt."

Annie took a deep breath and kept going. Now that she'd started talking about what happened, she couldn't stop.

"She made fun of my hair being long and scraggly and said my face was so hideous, it was no wonder I didn't wear any makeup because it would take two truckloads of it to cover my ugliness. The other two girls with her laughed a little. They looked uncomfortable, but they didn't tell her to stop. Amy was scared Carrie would start in on her, so she just sat there."

"What'd you do?" Truck asked softly.

"I wanted to hit her," Annie admitted.

"But you didn't," Truck said confidently.

"No," Annie mumbled. "But I threatened to. Told her she'd better hope I didn't see her after school because I was gonna beat the crap out of her."

Truck was silent, and Annie peeked up at him. She was slightly ashamed of what she'd said, but she wasn't sorry. Carrie deserved to be taken down a bit, and Annie wasn't scared of her. Not at all. She asked, "Aren't you going to tell me that was wrong? That I shouldn't have said that?"

"How long has this girl been picking on you?" Truck asked.

Annie shrugged. "Since the fourth grade," she said tentatively.

"And how many times have you told her to leave you alone? How many times have you ignored her taunts and all the mean things she's said to you?"

"Um...lots?" Annie said with a shrug.

"Sounds like she needs to be taken down a peg."

Annie stared at her dad's friend in confusion. Was he telling her it was *okay* to beat up Carrie?

"It seems to me as if you've given her way more chances than she deserves. Your mom would probably have a heart attack if she knew I was telling you this, but it's obvious Carrie thinks she's better than you. Which is bullshit—er...sorry...it's bullcrap. No one's better than you, Annie. Just as you aren't better than anyone else. This Carrie chick isn't going to leave you alone until you give her a *reason* to leave you alone."

Annie couldn't believe what she was hearing. But she couldn't deny she was relieved. "She told me her boyfriend was gonna be waiting for me after school. I managed to avoid him today, but I'm sure he'll be looking for me tomorrow," she admitted.

"See? She knows you'll kick her butt, so she's

sending someone else to do her dirty work. Can you take her boyfriend?" Truck asked.

Annie smiled. "Yes." She had no doubt whatsoever that she could totally win in a fight against Doug Chamberlin. He was taller than her, but he was all talk. He couldn't even climb the rope in gym class.

"Then do it," Truck said. "I'm not saying it'll shut stupid Carrie up forever, because I knew a lot of girls like her back when I was your age. But it'll make her think twice about picking on you in the near future. It'll also send a message that you won't tolerate people making fun of those weaker or different from everyone else. I'm proud of you for eating lunch with that boy today."

"I thought about Frankie. He told me how hard it was to adjust to the cochlear implant he got last year. All I could picture was him trying to make friends, self-conscious of the way he sounded when he talked, and no one sitting with him at lunch," Annie admitted.

"But Frankie's doing okay now?" Truck asked.

Annie nodded. "Yeah. He's awesome."

"Have you talked to him about what happened today?"

"Not yet."

"But you will?" Truck said.

Annie frowned. "Of course. Why wouldn't I?"

She didn't understand the small smile that formed on Truck's face. "No reason. You want to go to the backyard and practice some moves with me so you'll be ready for Doug and anything sneaky he might plan to take you off guard?"

"Yes!" Annie exclaimed immediately, feeling much better than she had a little while ago. She loved sparring with her dad and his friends. She knew they took it easy on her, but it was fun all the same. Someday, after she was a special forces soldier herself, she'd come home and kick their butts for real. They wouldn't need to go on easy on her just because she was smaller and not as strong as they were.

"Okay. But first I need a hug," Truck said, sitting up and holding out his arms.

Annie knew what he was doing. He didn't need a hug, but she had no doubt that he knew *she* needed one. Growing up was hard. She wasn't sure she liked it much. Her boobs had started to grow, which she hated. She'd learned all about puberty in her health class and how she'd soon start bleeding between her legs. She had a hard time controlling her emotions and she felt off-kilter all the time. Annie despised every minute of it.

Some people, like Carrie, wanted to grow up as fast as possible, but Annie liked being little. She enjoyed being doted on by her dad and his friends.

She liked not having to spend hours doing home-work, and not having to try very hard to get good grades. But as she got older, the schoolwork got harder, she was expected to spend more time thinking about her appearance and less time playing outside. Growing old sucked.

She crawled out of her closet and snuggled into Truck's lap. The man was huge, and he made her feel like she was little once more.

"I'm proud of the young woman you're becoming, Annie," Truck said. "Even though you're growing up way too fast. If you keep growing like you are, you're gonna be taller than me soon."

Annie giggled. "Whatever. You're a giant, Truck."

"You worried your mom," he said softly.

Annie closed her eyes. She had. She knew that. But she hadn't been able to stop herself from slam-ming her door and telling her to go away.

"And Ethan's wondering where his favorite sister is, why she didn't greet him when she got home."

Annie frowned. "Making me feel guilty is mean," she told Truck.

It was his turn to chuckle. She felt the rumble of his chest under her cheek.

"You're right. I'm sorry."

"No, *I'm* sorry. I just...sometimes I just feel all these emotions. And I can't control them. I was so *mad* when I got home. I didn't want to talk to anyone."

"I know," Truck soothed. His hand kept her close, and Annie swore his palm was so big it covered her entire back. "I think that's a part of being a teenager."

Annie shifted so she could see Truck's eyes. "Are you gonna tell Mom and Dad about what happened?"

Truck stared at her for a long moment, then he shook his head. "No. But that doesn't mean I don't think *you* should."

Annie sighed. "Mom's gonna want to go to the school and talk to the principal. You know how she is. And that's not going to help anything. It'll just make Carrie even worse. And if Fletch thinks someone wants to fight me, he'll lose his mind. I can take care of myself, but I'll always be seven to him."

"You know I feel the same way, right?" Truck asked with a small grin.

Annie returned it and shook her head. "No, you don't. If you did, you wouldn't tell me to beat Doug's ass into the ground."

Truck laughed. "True. But that doesn't mean I'm not protective of you."

Annie's grin faded. "I know. But I've learned from watching Fletch with my mom, that being protective isn't a bad thing. He feels the same way about her, and yet he still let's her do stuff. He doesn't smother her. Doesn't take over when he thinks she's making a mistake. That's what loving someone is about. Letting them do what they need to do, and being there for them afterward if it doesn't turn out like they thought it would."

"How'd you get so smart?" Truck asked.

"From being around you and the rest of Dad's friends. I see how you and everyone else is with your wives. You're protective, but you also love that they're independent. You wouldn't be happy with someone who couldn't make a decision for herself. Mary's perfect for you, and even though you worry about her, you don't stand in her way when she wants to do something. Like when she went skydiving with Harley the other month. It seemed like you were going to puke, but whenever Mary looked at you, you smiled and encouraged her."

"I *did* think I was going to puke. Do you know what happened the last time Harley went skydiving?" Truck asked.

Annie rolled her eyes. "Of course. I've heard the story a million times. A bird hit Coach in the face and knocked him out and she saved his life by guiding the parachute down."

"Right. You think I wanted that to happen to Mary?"

"No. But you still let her go," Annie insisted.

"You think Frankie will be that way with you?" Truck asked.

Annie appreciated the fact that he didn't hesitate to assume she and Frankie were going to get married and live happily ever after. Lots of adults thought she would "grow out of" wanting to be with him eventually, but Annie knew Frankie was the boy for her. They were meant to be with each other forever and ever.

"Yes," she said firmly.

"Me too," Truck said. "Now, how about we get up, you go hug your mom, say hi to Mary, reassure Ethan that you haven't forgotten about him, tell Fletch that you're all better now, and we eat some lasagna. Then after dinner, we'll go outside and make sure you're ready for whatever stupid Doug throws your way."

"I love you, Truck," Annie told him. And she did. She hadn't known what she was missing when it had been just her and Mom. She loved her mother more than anyone in the world, but the day Fletch and his friends came into their lives made everything even better.

They got up off the floor and headed into the kitchen together. Annie did as Truck suggested, hugging her mom and telling her that she was sorry for being a brat. Then she did the same to her dad.

She greeted Mary warmly, then sat on the couch with Ethan and took the book he held out to her. She'd read it to him a thousand times already, but she didn't mind reading it again.

Dinner was fantastic, as always, and afterward, Truck didn't show her any mercy when they faced off in the backyard. By the time he and Mary left, she was tired, sweaty, and more determined than ever to show Carrie and Doug that she wasn't someone to be messed with.

Fletch came into her room to tuck her into bed, which was unusual, as she'd stopped wanting to be tucked in a while ago. He didn't beat around the bush.

"You want to talk about it, sprite?"

Annie's heart beat fast. Had he figured out she was probably going to be in a fight tomorrow? "No," she said a little more breathlessly than she wanted.

Fletch stared at her for a long moment. Her dad always seemed to see right through her. He always knew when she was lying or hiding something from him. It was annoying.

He sighed, sitting on the side of her bed. "Fine. I know I'm just your old man. But whatever you do, don't let your emotions overcome your good sense."

Annie blinked up at him in surprise. Was he... giving her fighting advice?

"And you're relying too much on your dominant side. We need to work on your left-handed strikes and rolling left instead of always to the right. Your opponent will pick up on that quickly and take advantage. And anyone who knows what they're doing will try to use words to rile you up and make you lose control. Ignore any taunts and concentrate on what you're doing. It's always best to strike hard and fast and end the fight before it starts. I know firsthand that you can keep going if you're hurt—I've seen you do it often enough when you're on the obstacle course—but in hand-to-hand, it's harder to stay at full strength if someone gets in a lucky strike. Focus, get it done, and get out of there. Okay?"

For a long moment, Annie could only stare at her dad in shock.

"Um...okay," she finally managed to say. His advice was good. The last thing she wanted was someone calling for a teacher and getting her in trouble. Carrie had brought this on, and she wanted the girl's bullying to end here and now. Getting detention, and the fight being interrupted before she could make her point, wouldn't stop the popular girl. Annie needed to show her—and anyone she used to fight her battles for her—that Annie wasn't someone who would put up with bullying. Period.

"I love you, sprite. And I'd bet on *you* over any

pampered princess, or the boy who's trying to impress her, any day," Fletch said. Then he kissed her on the forehead and stood.

When he got to the doorway, Annie had recovered from her shock. Truck had obviously talked to Fletch at some point. She was fairly sure her dad hadn't said anything to her mom though, because there was no way her mom would be all right with Annie starting any kind of fight. No matter if it was the right thing to do or not. "Dad?" she said softly.

"Yeah?" Fletch asked as he turned to look at her. The light from the hallway made him look like a giant black blob, but Annie knew without a doubt that he was looking at her with love in his eyes. He always had.

"Thank you for not being mad," she said softly.

"I'd only be mad if you were fighting just because someone said something bad about you. But I know you, Annie. You don't care what others say about you, you only care when they pick on someone else. Next time, though, I hope you'll talk about it with *me*."

Annie wanted to cry. Fletch was awesome. "I will," she told him.

"Good. Kick some bully butt tomorrow, sprite. We'll tell your mom about it together. Get some sleep." Then he shut the door behind him quietly, leaving Annie in the dark, counting her lucky stars that her mom had met and married an amazing guy like Fletch.

———————

As it turned out, the fight the next day was over almost as soon as it began. Doug, Carrie, and three of her posse cornered Annie in the hallway outside the gym before seventh period. Doug shoved her and said a lot of stupid shit about how her dad was enlisted and she was dirt.

Annie rolled her eyes and took a step toward him, rather than cowering away, which obviously surprised him. Carrie must've lied and told him how scared Annie would be.

Then Annie swung, hitting him in the face.

Doug's eyes went wide and he stumbled back with one hand covering his cheek, where's she'd hit him. Before he recovered, Annie shoved him, *hard*, and he hit the wall behind him, losing his balance and falling to his butt on the tiles.

Annie glared at him and narrowed his eyes. "My dad might be enlisted, but he's also special forces—and he taught me how to fight dirty. You want to see what else he taught me?" she asked.

In response, Doug got to his feet and quickly walked away.

Carrie called out his name, but he ignored her. Annie smirked, got up in Carrie's face and told her if she ever came within ten feet of her again, or anyone she considered a friend, and tried to talk smack, she'd stop being so polite.

Carrie and her girl posse practically ran away.

All in all, Annie didn't exactly feel good about what had happened, but it was satisfying to stand up for herself, and to get a bit of revenge for anyone who'd been bullied by the mean girl in the past.

When she walked in her front door after school, to her surprise, Fletch was there. His gaze roamed her from head to toe, then, satisfied that she was in one piece, he nodded proudly.

"Hey, honey," her mom said. "How was school?"

"It was good, Mom," Annie said. Instead of going to Ethan, as she usually did, Annie walked right up to Fletch. She hugged him hard.

"You good?"

Annie nodded as she looked up at him.

"*They* good?" he asked with a small smile.

Annie couldn't help but giggle.

"Who's they?" her mom asked.

"Yeah," Annie told Fletch. "Wasn't much of anything. Especially once he found out my special forces dad taught me everything he knew."

It was Fletch's turn to chuckle. "That's my girl.

How about you go and say hello to your brother and give me a minute with your mom."

Annie nodded and squeezed Fletch one more time before wandering into the living room.

"What's going on?" her mom asked.

Annie heard Fletch talking to her mom, but she couldn't hear all the words. She wasn't worried though. Fletch would make everything all right.

Annie was proud of herself. She didn't want to fight, but standing up for herself felt great. As did having the confidence knowing she could hold her own against a boy older, taller, and stronger than she was.

That night, no one brought up what happened at school. Her mom was her usual happy self, and when Ethan threw a fit at the table because he wanted more French fries instead of eating the green beans their mom had put on his plate, Annie was able to calm him down by telling him green beans would make him grow up big and strong like her.

But she wasn't surprised when her mom knocked on her door after she'd gone up to bed.

"Come in," Annie called out.

Emily came in and sat on her bed, much as Fletch had done the night before. "You okay, baby?" her mom asked.

"Yeah."

"You need some ice for that hand?"

Annie shouldn't be surprised her mom had noticed the scrape on her knuckles, or that she'd been babying her right hand a bit throughout dinner. "It'll be okay," she told her.

Emily sighed. "For the record, I don't like fighting."

Annie held her breath, waiting for the lecture she was sure was coming. Until her mom surprised her with her next words.

"But I'm so proud of you for sticking up for yourself. You're never going to be like other little girls. I knew that from the time you were two and threw a fit when I tried to put you in a dress and you wanted to wear pants. You never do what society expects of a girl, and yet, you have the most tender and considerate heart of anyone I've ever met. All I've ever wanted is for you to be a good person and to strive for whatever it is your heart desires."

"Thanks, Mom," Annie said softly.

"Fletch told me what happened, and I have to say...Carrie's a bitch."

Annie couldn't stop the snort from escaping.

"I know I shouldn't say that, as I'm an adult and she's a kid. But seriously, she's been on your case for years, and for what? Because you don't wear makeup and can outrun and climb everyone in your class?

Anyway, I don't like that you have to resort to using your fists, but I hope she got the message today."

"I hope so too," Annie said.

"I'm never going to stop worrying about you," her mom said. "Especially when you're in the special forces and on missions saving the world. I'll be proud as hell—but I'll never stop worrying."

Her mom's unwavering belief that Annie would someday be a special forces soldier felt good. Really good. "Thanks," she whispered.

"Love you, baby."

"Love you too, Mom."

"See you in the morning." With that, her mom leaned down, kissed Annie's forehead, and left the room.

Smiling, Annie reached for her phone. She couldn't wait to tell Frankie all about what happened. And that her mom hadn't freaked out. She'd texted him right after the fight, if it could even be called that, but she couldn't wait to tell him in person how awesome she'd been.

* * *

Fletch held Emily tight as they sat on the back deck. There wasn't a cloud in the sky and while it wasn't exactly warm, it wasn't cold either. And with a blanket thrown over them, and Fletch's body heat, he was confident his wife wasn't cold.

"You okay?" he asked.

Emily nodded, but said, "No. I don't like that she's getting into fights. What if this continues? What if she gets suspended? Joins a gang? Starts beating up people for fun?"

Fletch couldn't help but laugh. "She won't," he said, once he had himself under control.

"You don't know that," Emily protested.

"I do. Because Annie didn't get in that fight today because Carrie was picking on her. She did it because she'd had enough of that little bitch going after those who are weaker. Kids like that new boy in class. The handicapped one. Our daughter is going to be a hell of a soldier. She's gonna make it, Em. I have no doubt."

Emily sighed against him. "It's not what I wanted for her."

"I know," Fletch said. And he did. Because he felt the same way. Annie didn't have an easy road ahead of her. She was going to have to work twice as hard as any other man to make any kind of special forces team. She'd be ridiculed, talked down to, looked down upon, and overlooked time and time again, simply because of her gender.

But Fletch had a feeling all of that would only

make her more hungry. Being told she wasn't good enough would make her work harder to prove people wrong. And just like Carrie and the boy she'd convinced to do her dirty work had found out, others would quickly learn not to underestimate Annie.

"I'm not sure I'm going to survive her teenage years," Emily said.

"We will," Fletch assured her. "When she gets grumpy, we'll throw Ethan at her. She loves that kid, and there's no way she can be around him and be in a bad mood."

"True," Emily mused.

"Besides, she'll be busy with the other kids we're going to have as well," Fletch told her.

"Four years apart," Emily reminded him. "Seriously, I need the break between them."

"I haven't forgotten," Fletch said. He didn't care how much time passed between their children. He would even be content if they didn't have any others. Emily, Ethan, and Annie had made his life so much more complete than he ever could've imagined.

"Frankie's good for her," Emily mused out of the blue.

"He is," Fletch agreed.

"You think they're going to make it?"

"Yes."

"Me too," Emily agreed. She glanced up at him.

"If someone would've asked me five years ago if I thought my life could be this good, I would've said no way. I was struggling to raise Annie as a single mother, and I couldn't imagine ever meeting someone who loves us as much as you do."

"I thought I'd be single forever," Fletch agreed. "Then a little sprite snuck under my shields and cracked my heart wide open."

Emily smiled.

"Seriously. You have no idea how much I love you and our kids," Fletch said. "No matter what the future holds with Annie, Ethan, and any other children we might have. In sickness and in health. I'll never love anyone the way I love you, Em."

"Don't make me cry," she ordered, ducking her head and snuggling against him.

Fletch smiled against her hair. "Sorry," he murmured.

They sat cuddled together for another fifteen minutes before Emily stirred. "I need to finish putting the dishes away. And make a grocery list for tomorrow. And fold clothes."

"I have a better idea," Fletch said, easily standing with his wife in his arms.

"Yeah?" she asked.

"Yup. I'm thinking we need to practice making our next baby. Even though it'll be a while before you go off your birth control, I wouldn't want to get rusty. Remember how fun it was when we were trying to conceive Ethan?" he asked.

Emily chuckled as he carried her into the house, making sure the door was locked behind them before heading for their bedroom.

"Fletch, I swear you got me pregnant the first month I went off birth control. There wasn't much 'trying' involved."

"But we didn't know that would happen," he told her.

"True," Emily said with a small smile, obviously remembering how many times they'd made love once they'd decided to try for a baby.

Fletch had taken her over and over, filling her with his come every night and most mornings. It had been one of the most erotic times in his life, not knowing if and when his sperm would take root in her beautiful body. He loved sex with his wife at all times, but that period before they'd learned he'd knocked her up, with him doing his level best to make sure it happened, made them both insatiable.

"I'm not sure I'll survive that again," Emily said with a sigh.

"Yes, you will," Fletch told her. "You just need a reminder of how awesome it was." He felt her squirm against him. Yeah, she was as turned on as he was just thinking about making a baby.

"You're right," she agreed.

Fletch lowered her legs until her feet hit the ground next to their bed. He took her face in his hands and tilted it up to his. "I love you, Emily. So much, sometimes it's scares me. I knew what Annie was going to do today, and if I'd had even one iota of a doubt that she wouldn't be able to kick that punk-ass kid's ass, I would've stopped it. The thought of her getting hurt makes me literally sick. But she's going to be in the military. I want to make sure she has the confidence of knowing she can take care of herself."

"I know," Emily said softly.

"And for the record, if we have another girl...I'm gonna go overboard with pink, and dolls, and girly shit, so I don't have to go through this again. I couldn't concentrate on *anything* today. All I could think about was Annie and what might be happening."

Emily laughed. "My big tough Delta Force soldier. Brought to his knees by his daughter."

"Yup," Fletch said without any shame.

"Make love to me," Emily whispered.

Fletch didn't respond verbally, he simply reached for the hem of her shirt and lifted it up and over her head. As he stared down at the woman who'd stolen his heart, he couldn't imagine his life without her by his side.

Whatever the future held, with Annie, Ethan, and any other children they might have, his rock was this woman. Together, they'd get through anything.

* * *

I just love Annie. I hope you will love seeing her all grown up in her very own full length book...*Rescuing Annie.*

Sign up for my newsletter to receive info on all my new releases here:
https://www.stokeraces.com/contact-1.html

TEX MEETS AKILAH

by Susan Stoker

ABOUT THE BOOK

Tex was used to watching over military men and women all over the world. But when he got a call about an orphaned Iraqi teenager who is on her way to the States and would be having her arm amputated as soon as she got here...everything except getting to the girl was put on the back burner.

Read the story of how Tex and Akilah met and how she captured the Veteran SEAL's heart without even trying.

TEX MEETS AKILAH

"TEX. It's Doctor Joiner. I just put a patient on a flight headed for Pittsburgh. She needed care that we couldn't provide here in Iraq."

John "Tex" Keegan frowned in confusion. He knew a lot of people. Had contacts all over the world. But he hadn't expected to hear from one of the United Nations surgeons he'd gotten to know over the years. A man who was vital in keeping Tex informed about any injuries the men and women he had on his radar might suffer while deployed.

"Who?" he asked, his adrenaline spiking. His mind spun, wondering which soldier the doctor was talking about. He'd said "she," and as far as he knew, none of the women he kept his eye on were in Baghdad.

"Her name is Akilah. We don't know her last

name. The neighborhood she lived in was bombed by the fucking Taliban. Casualties were high."

Tex nodded, although he was still confused about why Dr. Joiner had called him.

"She's twelve," the doctor said softly. "From what little information the team who brought her in could get, both of her parents were killed in the bombing. Her not dying is literally a miracle. She's gonna lose her arm though, Tex. It's bad. As I said earlier, I don't have the skills to help her in the way she needs, if she's going to be able to live any kind of normal life in the future. So I'm sending her to the States. To you."

Most men would probably protest. Ask the doctor what the hell he was thinking. Tex wasn't a medic. He was already up to his eyeballs looking after others. Making sure they were safe. Organizing assistance when needed. Doing whatever he could to keep his friends safe.

But the moment Tex heard the girl's name...something clicked deep within him. And knowing she was going to be an amputee, like him, sealed the deal. "When is she arriving?" he asked the doctor.

The relief in the man's voice was easy to hear as he replied, "Tonight. She'll immediately head to surgery. She doesn't speak English, so that's going to be a challenge."

"I'll find a translator," Tex said. "Someone who

can sit with her and explain everything that's going on." He couldn't imagine how scary this must be for that little girl. To be living her life and suddenly have it explode around her, killing everyone she knew and loved. Then to be brought to a hospital, in pain, and put on a plane to God knows where.

Yes, Tex's first priority was finding someone who spoke her language, who could reassure her and comfort her when everything became too much.

"She's going to need a sponsor," the doctor warned.

Tex laughed. "Which is why you called me, is it not?"

But the doctor didn't laugh. "There's something about her..." he began. "Even in the midst of everything going on, she simply stared at me as if she could read my mind. As if she knew I was trying to help her. I pulled a lot of strings to get her out of the country. Doctors here in Baghdad could've probably amputated her arm, but then what? Where would she go? What would she do? We both know what the quality of her life would be. Anyway...I just emailed you a picture of her," Doctor Joiner said, a moment before Tex's program dinged, letting him know he'd received the email.

Tex opened it and clicked on the picture attached. A girl was lying on a stretcher, staring up at the camera. Her eyes were dark brown, her hair the same shade, except it was covered in a sheen of dust. Her face was dirty, pain etched into her expression, but Tex saw what the doctor was talking about.

A resilience that he rarely saw anymore, deep in her gaze. This girl had clearly seen more than her share of suffering and struggles, and yet...hope still shone from her depths of her soul. Hope for a better future. Hope that someone would help her.

Tex stared at her picture for a full minute before he was able to speak.

"I've got this," he said in a firm voice.

"Thank you," Doctor Joiner said.

"No, thank *you*," Tex returned. "I've got to go. I have a lot of work to do to get ready for Akilah's arrival. But if there's anything you need, *anything*, you let me know."

"The mighty Tex offering me a marker?" the doctor asked, finally laughing.

Tex didn't feel a need to respond. Most of the people he worked with knew they could call him if they required assistance. But it was rare for Tex to give someone carte blanche for literally any help they might need.

"I wouldn't mind an update on how she's doing," the doctor said.

"That's a given," Tex said. "I'll be in touch."

"Appreciate it. Later."

Tex hung up and looked at the picture once more. He didn't know what it was about the girl that called so strongly to him, but there was no way he could ignore it. Taking a deep breath, Tex clicked on the print icon and his printer begin to whirl. He needed to talk to Melody. Then make sure the translation app on his phone had Arabic as one of the languages provided. He'd never been so glad for technology as he was right at that moment. He still needed to find a translator, but he also wanted to be able to talk to the girl one-on-one, and the app would allow him to do that.

Standing, he grabbed the picture off the printer and headed upstairs to find his wife.

————

Later the following evening, after hiring and sending an older native Iraqi woman to the hospital to be with Akilah, Tex picked up his phone.

"Tex! What do I owe this pleasure?" the man on the other end said when he answered.

"I need a favor, Wolf."

There was silence on the other end for a moment, as if he'd surprised his old friend.

"You got it," Wolf said. "Melody all right?"

"Yes."

"Baby?"

Baby was their three-legged coonhound who was as much a part of his family as any child might be. "She's good," Tex reassured him. He quickly explained the situation with Akilah, then got to the reason he was calling. "I need a letter of recommendation. Addressed to Akilah, keeping in mind that she's only twelve. I want her to trust me. To know that I'm going to do whatever it takes to keep her safe."

"When do you need it by?" Wolf asked.

"Oh-seven hundred," Tex said.

Wolf chuckled. "Jeez, way to give me some advanced warning."

"She's having surgery tonight. I want to be by her side when she wakes up tomorrow. And I want to make sure she knows that I have nothing but her best interests in mind."

"Don't take this the wrong way...but why?" Wolf asked. "You've helped countless people. Children included. What makes her different?"

"She's mine," Tex said. "Don't ask how I know that, I just do."

To his credit, his SEAL friend didn't question him further.

"It'll be in your inbox before twenty-four hundred," Wolf told him.

"I owe you."

"The hell you do," Wolf countered. "Have you forgotten what you've done for me? For Caroline? For my team? You don't owe me a damn thing."

Tex's throat got tight. He didn't do what he did for thanks. In fact, he hated when people thanked him just for being a decent human being. For doing his part to fight the evil in the world. But knowing his friend had his back without questioning his feelings for this little girl he hadn't even met...it meant the world.

"I'm going to want to meet her," Wolf continued.

"Done." Tex wanted the *world* to meet his daughter.

His daughter.

He was getting ahead of himself. And he knew most people would think he was crazy for wanting to bring Akilah into his life. But the second he'd shown her picture to Melody and explained the situation, she'd been one hundred precent committed to bringing her home, just as he was. Not that he'd had any doubt she'd feel the same way. They'd always been on the same wavelength.

"Gotta go," Tex said. "I've got more calls to make."

"If you and Mel need any help, just give us a yell. I'm sure Caroline would love to make a trip out there to see you...and help with anything you might need when you bring Akilah home."

Tex smiled. "Will do."

"I'll get that letter to you soon. Talk to you later."

Tex hung up with Wolf, then immediately dialed another number. Calling his friend Ghost, who was in the Army and lived in Texas. Fifteen minutes later, after repeating the conversation he'd had with Wolf, and Ghost promising his wife, Rayne, would also fly out to help if they needed it, Tex hung up.

The calls continued. To a man a lot like him who lived in Colorado. To Mustang, a SEAL out in Hawaii. To Rocco, a SEAL in California. To Ethan "Chaos" Watson, a former special forces member who now led a search and rescue team in Fallport, Virginia. To Drake "Brick" Vandine, a man a lot like Tex, a former SEAL who had a three-legged mutt, and who was currently living in New Mexico running a retreat called The Refuge, for men and women who needed a break from the world and the demons nipping at their heels.

Tex called everyone he could think of. He wanted Akilah to trust him. *Needed* her to. And the only way he could think of to make that happen was to have people he trusted reassure her that he was a good guy. That he had her best interests at heart.

By the time he hung up the phone for the last time, Tex was exhausted. He knew he wouldn't be able to sleep. Not when he was worried about Akilah and her surgery. He'd been where she was once. When he'd had his own leg amputated, he'd been scared shitless. Worried what would become of his life. Wondered what the hell he was going to do now.

But he'd been a grown-ass man. Not a child who'd lost her entire family and was now in a foreign country where she didn't speak the language. Akilah was going to need a lot of reassurance and a lot of love and patience. Something he and Melody had in spades.

The worst day in young Akilah's life could turn out to be a new beginning...if she'd let them into her life.

Tex stood, arched his back and groaned at the feel of his bones cracking. He was getting older, and while he'd loved having Melody to himself, he was ready for more. For a family.

He took a step toward the door, needing to see his wife, and grimaced. His leg was hurting. He'd been wearing his prosthetic for too long. As he headed up the stairs, everything Tex wanted to teach

Akilah about the prosthetic she'd eventually get raced through his brain.

First and foremost, he wanted to make sure she knew that losing an arm didn't mean she was any less valuable as a person. She could overcome the disability and show the world that she was just as strong and capable as anyone else.

Melody had done that for him. She hadn't even blinked at the sight of his mangled leg or his prosthetic. She'd shown him it was who he was inside that mattered. Tex wanted to do the same for Akilah.

Making sure his phone was turned on so he wouldn't miss the call from the head surgeon, who'd promised to be in touch the second he was done working on Akilah, Tex pushed open the door at the top of the steps that led out of the basement. Melody was sitting in their living room, Baby at her side, the dog's head on her lap and eyes closed. His wife was reading a book, soft music playing from the television.

His love for her was nearly overwhelming. Tex had never thought he could love anyone as much as he loved his wife. She was his everything. Without her, he wouldn't be able to do what he did. She was his inspiration and his reason for fighting so hard to keep his friends and their families safe.

"Everything okay?" she asked quietly.

He wasn't surprised she knew he was there, despite how quietly he moved. They had a sixth sense when it came to each other. Tex walked toward the couch, not trying to hide his limp.

"Yeah. Everyone agreed to write a letter."

"Of course they did," Melody said as she stood. Baby groaned at losing her pillow, but immediately rolled onto her back, her three legs in the air as she closed her eyes and sighed.

Tex chuckled. It was hard to believe looking at the lazy hound right now that she'd ever ferociously attacked someone. She'd been protecting him and Mel, and had been shot in the process. The dog *deserved* a lazy life.

"Come on, you need to get off that leg," Melody said matter-of-factly. "I'll get the lotion to massage it while you rest."

Fuck, he loved this woman. He went to her and pulled her into his embrace. "I don't deserve you," he said softly. "I spend too much time in the basement. I forget to eat. I don't do enough around the house."

"I love you exactly how you are. I love that you work so hard to help others. You were there when I needed you, so I know exactly how others in my same situation, or worse, feel. I can mow the grass and do housework without your help. And if need be, I can pick up the phone and call someone to fix the toilet or install a ceiling fan. You just keep on being you and we'll be just fine."

She turned, kept one arm around his waist, and headed for the hallway that led to their bedroom.

"Are you sure about Akilah?" Tex couldn't help but ask. "She's going to require a therapist. And her other medical needs won't be cheap."

They were in their bedroom now, and Melody turned once more to face him. She put her hands on his cheeks and leaned in. "She needs us," she said simply. "I'm sure. We'll figure it out together. All of us."

"She might decide she doesn't want to stay in the US," Tex warned. He'd been thinking about that a lot. Once she was healed and had her prosthetic, she might choose to go back to Iraq. And he wouldn't blame her. It was her home country. The only place she'd known.

Melody shrugged. "She might. But that doesn't mean that she won't have our support."

That was true.

"I love you," he said.

"And I love you back. Now, get changed and I'll get the stuff from the bathroom. I want you on the bed, prosthetic off by the time I return."

Tex smiled. "Yes, ma'am."

Melody leaned up and kissed him. It was long,

56

slow, and deep, and all of a sudden, Tex wasn't tired anymore.

She grinned. "After we take care of your leg," she said, as if she knew exactly what he was thinking. And she probably did. Melody winked confidently at him, then turned and headed for the bathroom. Her hips swaying enticingly.

Melody was the only person who could pull him out of his own head. When he was worried about whoever he was tracking at the moment, or whatever latest disaster was unfolding, she was the one who made sure he ate and drank. Made sure he took care of himself, as he was taking care of everyone else.

She'd make an excellent mother.

They'd talked about children before, but the time had never seemed right. With the prospect of Akilah joining their family...maybe it was time to start thinking about babies again. Melody was the most nurturing, caring woman he'd ever known.

"You aren't on the bed," she scolded when she reentered the room.

Tex jolted in surprise. He'd been so deep in his head, imaging Melody as a mother, that he was still standing where he'd been when she walked away.

"Sorry," he muttered as he quickly limped to the bed. He shucked off his pants and Melody helped remove his prosthetic. He couldn't help the erection that formed as she massaged his stump. Every time she put her hands on him *anywhere*, he had the same reaction.

Melody had a small smile on her face, but she didn't rush through her ministrations. When she was finished, she wiped the lotion off her hands and studied him. "Feel better?" she asked.

"Much," Tex told her. "Come here," he ordered, holding his arms out.

She snuggled against him, and Tex held her tightly for a long moment. When she lifted her head, he could read the lust in her eyes.

She straddled his waist and gazed down at him. "I love you."

"Love you too, Mel."

The next thirty minutes were spent showing each other exactly how deeply their love ran. When they were both exhausted, slightly sweaty, and replete from their orgasms, Melody was once more lying in Tex's arms.

He turned his head and kissed her temple reverently.

"You gonna be able to sleep?" Melody murmured.

"Yeah," he said, and he actually wasn't lying. He was worried about Akilah and anxious about missing the doctor's call. He needed to print off the emails his friends had all promised, check in with the translator, and look into everything that might be required to bring Akilah home...but for the moment, he was content to doze in his wife's arms.

————

The next morning, Tex was amazed that he'd been able to sleep as long as he had. The surgeon had called around three-thirty in the morning to let him know the surgery had gone extremely well. Akilah had endured a transhumeral amputation, meaning above the elbow. She was recovering well so far, and she'd be awake and aware in the morning, when Tex would be able to see her.

He'd gotten up about an hour and a half after the call and printed the letters his friends had sent—and they'd come through in a big way. Not only had each man he'd called written a letter, but all of their teammates had, as well, as did many of their wives. He had dozens of letters to share with Akilah, in the hopes they'd help her understand he had only her best interests at heart.

Melody had wanted to go with him to the hospital, but she hadn't wanted to overwhelm the girl as soon as she woke up. There would be plenty of time for his wife to meet the girl who would hopefully become a permanent part of their lives.

Taking a deep breath, Tex entered the hospital. It wasn't a place that held good memories for him. It didn't matter that he hadn't been in *this* hospital, they all smelled and sounded the same. Pushing the bad memories away, he headed for the fourth floor, where the doctor told him Akilah would be.

He knocked briefly and heard a female voice he assumed belonged to the translator, telling him to enter. He pushed the door open slowly—and froze at the sight of the girl on the bed. Her hair was in disarray around her head. She had tubes sticking out of her good arm, and bandages were wrapped around the stump of the other.

But it was her eyes that made Tex pause.

They were so full of pain, it was all he could do not to rush across the room and wrap his arms around her.

Forcing himself to move slowly, so as not to alarm the girl, Tex walked farther into the room.

"Good morning," the older woman said quietly.

Tex nodded. "I'm Tex," he told her.

"It's nice to meet you."

"Everything okay?" he asked the translator, no time for niceties. He wanted to talk to Akilah. Reassure her that she was safe.

"Yes. Akilah woke up about two hours ago. She hasn't eaten much, but the doctors say that's normal."

Tex nodded, his gaze was drawn back to Akilah. She hadn't taken her eyes from him. He pulled up a chair on the opposite side of the bed from the translator. "Has she said much?" he asked, staring into Akilah's eyes.

"No. But she does seem to be more relaxed now that I'm here to translate for her."

"Good." He forced himself to look at the woman. "Thank you for taking the job on such short notice."

The woman snorted. "First, I would've been stupid to turn it down, considering how generously you're paying me. Second, this poor girl is all alone, and I can't imagine what she's been though. Third, I realize she doesn't know me, but having someone from the same part of the world as she's from has to be a comfort."

Tex pulled his phone out of his pocket and pulled up the document he'd put together that morning. He looked at the woman. "Will you please translate for me?"

"Of course."

Tex took a deep breath and looked back at Akilah. She hadn't moved an inch, was still staring at him as if she was waiting for him to either hurt her or give her bad news.

He spoke slowly, giving the woman time to translate his words as he recited a greeting.

"Hello, Akilah. My name is John Keegan. Most people call me Tex. I'm so sorry for all you've been through. I'm sure you've been told, but you're in the United States. In Pennsylvania. My wife and I live not too far from this hospital. How are you feeling?"

He didn't take his gaze from hers as she spoke, and the woman translated. "Tired. Sad. Scared."

Tex nodded. "I'm not surprised. You've been through a lot."

"My parents are dead."

Tex wasn't sure if she was trying to shock him with her words or if she was simply stating a fact, but he kept his face neutral. "I'm so very sorry."

"My friend was raped. I hid so they couldn't find me, but they found her and hurt her. Then they shot her. I was too scared to come out. Then the bombs came."

Tex's heart literally broke for the girl. He wanted to touch her. Hold her hand. But after everything she'd seen and been through, he didn't think she'd want him, a stranger, touching her. "You're safe here," he told her quietly.

For the first time, Akilah closed her eyes. She also turned her head away from him.

Her reaction tore Tex's heart in two. He regretted not insisting Melody come along with him. He wasn't good at this kind of thing. Swallowing hard, he held out the phone to the translator. "Will you read this to her, after I explain what she's about to hear?"

The woman nodded. Tex could see tears in her eyes too. Akilah was surrounded by people who cared about her...himself, the translator, the doctors and nurses...but she was too scared and hurt to see it. She would though. He'd do whatever it took to make her feel safe.

"Akilah, will you please look at me?" he asked.

After the woman had translated, Akilah turned her head back toward him and met his gaze.

"Thank you. You don't know me, and I know you're scared. You're in a new country, don't speak the language, and are probably in a lot of pain. But I'm here because I care about you. A United Nations doctor called me and told me about you. He purposely sent you to this hospital for your surgery because he knew I lived nearby. I'm going to do everything in my power to make sure you're safe while you heal. When the doctor says it's okay, I'd like to bring you to my home to continue your recovery."

Akilah's brow furrowed, and he could read the question in her eyes without her having to say a word.

"You want to know why. Why would a complete stranger care about a girl from Iraq, a country the

United States was essentially at war with not too long ago."

The confusion turned to surprise.

Tex ignored that and continued. "It's because I loathe injustice. And violence against innocent women and children is something I'll never stand for. You didn't deserve what happened to you and I'm in a position to help you overcome it."

Akilah didn't look convinced.

"I don't expect you to immediately trust me," Tex reassured her. "In fact, I'm somewhat relieved you don't. That's smart. Because you don't know me, I asked my friends to write you letters, explaining why you can trust me. That if you let me into your life, you won't regret it. I didn't alter their letters in any way. I didn't change one word. Will you listen to them before you make your decision?"

Akilah looked tired, but this was important. He wanted her trust. Needed it. He couldn't explain it, but the feeling wouldn't go away.

After one of the longest moments of Tex's life, Akilah nodded.

"Thank you," he said quietly, then nodded at the translator.

She cleared her throat and began speaking.

"Akilah, my name is Wolf. I've known Tex for many years. He literally saved my wife's life. More than once. Tex absolutely refused to give up when she was lost and no one else could find her. I know you're probably scared right now, but Tex has your back. I trust him with the most valuable thing in my life...my wife.

"Dear Akilah, my name is Fiona. I'm married to a Navy SEAL, and we live out in California. You are one lucky girl to have Tex as a champion. I was kidnapped and hidden away deep in the jungle. I didn't know Tex then, but as soon as he found out about me, he went out of his way to reassure my now-husband that no matter what, no one would ever take me again. I still get scared sometimes, but knowing Tex is out there, and will always come for me if something bad happens, makes me feel a lot better.

"Akilah. Hi! My name is Annie. I'm eight years old. My daddy is in the Army and he says that even though Tex was in the Navy, he's still one of the bestest people he's ever known. I think so too. He even let me beat him on the obstacle course once. His bionic leg is super cool, and you'll be getting a bionic arm and be just like Tex. He's nice and funny and if my mommy hadn't married Daddy Fletch, I wouldn't mind Tex as my daddy.

"Akilah. My name is Ethan. I live in Virginia, in a small town called Fallport. I used to be in the military, but now my job is to go into the forest and find people when they get lost. I'm sorry about what happened to you, but you couldn't find a better person to have at your side than Tex. Once, when I was far from home, I'd been hurt. I was in a hospital and feeling lonely and scared. You know what happened? I received a huge bouquet of flowers. From Tex. Even though I wasn't in the United States, Tex still knew what happened, and those flowers made me realize I wasn't alone. That I had friends. Let Tex be your friend, Akilah. I swear you won't regret it."

The translator continued reading the letters, but Tex didn't take his gaze from Akilah. She was staring at the woman as she read, and with every short note from his friends, she seemed to relax a tiny bit more.

After reading the final letter, the translator handed the phone back to Tex as Akilah asked something. The woman smiled at the girl and responded. Then she looked over at Tex. "She wanted to know what I thought. If I trusted you. I told her absolutely yes."

"Thank you," Tex said.

Akilah spoke again, and Tex looked at her. She looked worried.

"She wants you to know that she's missing her arm."

"I know," Tex said evenly.

"She says that she's...useless... Sorry, there's no direct translation for the word she used."

"You are *not* useless," Tex told Akilah firmly.

Akilah flinched, and Tex did his best to calm himself. The last thing he wanted was to freak the girl out. "Not having an arm doesn't mean you're any less than anyone else. It's just an arm."

Akilah responded, and Tex looked at the woman when she didn't immediately translate. "What'd she say?"

"You have to understand," she started, instead of translating. "Your culture is very different from hers. Imperfection is frowned upon. She comes from a male-dominated society and if a woman has any kind of flaw, they're seen as undesirable. Which means no one will want to marry her, and her life becomes much harder because she'll be at the mercy of many, since she doesn't have a husband. It's just a fact of life."

"Thank you for explaining. You can take a break now," Tex told the woman.

She looked surprise. "Oh, but don't you want me to translate?"

"Not right this moment. I'd like some time alone with Akilah."

She looked extremely skeptical, but she didn't protest. She said something to Akilah, probably that she'd be back later, then turned and left the room. Once the door was shut behind her, Tex immediately had second thoughts. He wouldn't be able to tell Akilah what he wanted, since he didn't speak Arabic. But he'd come a long way since he'd been injured... and this was something that was just between him and Akilah.

He stood and slowly began to roll up the leg of his pants, exposing his prosthetic. "I used to think the same way as you. When I lost my leg, I thought that was it. My life was over. I was a useless former SEAL who couldn't walk, couldn't kick ass the way I used to. I never thought I'd ever meet anyone who would see past my disability. There will always be people who look down on me because of this," he said, tapping his metal leg. "But fuck them. My brain works just fine and I've done my best over the years to prove that I'm just as capable as anyone else.

"You aren't useless, Akilah. Far from it. You'll learn to do things one-handed. You'll compensate for the loss of your arm. You can use your mind and show all the doubters that you're a hell of a young lady. Eventually, you'll meet someone who loves you for who you are. Not for what you look like or how many limbs you have. Someone like my Melody. Someone like my friends. Someone loyal, loving, protective, and who loves you unconditionally."

Tex knew he was babbling, knew Akilah couldn't understand him, but he couldn't help it. There was so much he wanted her to know. He couldn't exactly go to Iraq and find the terrorist assholes who had turned this girl's life upside down, but he *could* make sure she overcame what had happened to her and was stronger as a result.

He was about to call the translator back in so she could talk to Akilah, but then the girl lifted her hand and touched his prosthetic. She looked up at him and said something. Tex simply stared at her for a moment—then realized he was an idiot. He had the app that would translate for them. It was probably not very accurate, but it should do.

He fumbled with his phone and pulled up the app. Then he said, "I have a program that will translate our words until we can understand each other." He pushed the button to play his words back in Arabic, and he couldn't help but feel satisfaction course through him when Akilah's eyes lit up in wonder.

She nodded. Tex held the button down and moved the phone closer, then nodded encouragingly. She said something, and Tex played it back. The computerized voice recited her translated words.

"You have missing a leg."

He was right, the translation was crap, but Tex

could still understand her meaning. He smiled at her and nodded.

They communicated that way for several minutes. It was slow and cumbersome, but the joy on Akilah's face that she could talk directly to him was worth any amount of frustration with the technology. He told her how scared he'd been when he'd woken up without his leg. He talked about Melody and how incredible she was. He made sure to tell Akilah that while it would be a challenge not to have one of her limbs, it didn't mean she was any less worthy.

In turn, she told him she missed the stray dog she used to sneak food to in her neighborhood. She missed her friends and worried about what had happened to them. She admitted she was scared and confused.

Twenty minutes later, Tex felt as if he'd made great strides with the preteen. He'd reassured her that it was normal to be scared, but he was there to look out for her, would make sure nothing bad happened to her.

"Am I home going?" she asked through the app.

Tex met her gaze as he said, "That's up to you. What you do from here on out is your decision. I'd like for you to stay here for a while, at least until you're completely healed. You can come live with me and Melody...and our dog. I'm going to arrange for the best prosthetic I can find for you. I have no doubt you'll learn English in no time. But after you're healed, if you still want to go back to your country, I'll find a sponsor there for you and we'll get you home."

The words almost hurt to say, but Tex would never, ever, keep her from going back to Iraq if that's what she wanted. He'd have to be satisfied with whatever time she gave them in the meantime.

"You not lie?" she asked.

"I'll never lie to you," Tex reassured her.

"You want me?" she asked, as if she couldn't believe what he was saying.

Tex wondered if the app was translating correctly. So he made it as clear as he could. "I want you to be my daughter, Akilah. I want you to live with me and my wife. I want to teach you how to deal with your amputation. I want you to meet all my friends who wrote those letters. I want to give you everything."

Her eyes filled with tears, and for a second, Tex panicked. He was about to leap up and find the translator when Akilah put her hand on his. While they'd been talking, Tex had rested an arm on her bed, and the feel of her warm hand on his own made goose bumps race along his forearm.

"Yes," she said in English.

Tex smiled at her. He covered her hand with his

and they sat like that for a long while, not saying a word. But they didn't need words. Tex prayed she felt a glimmer of the same connection he felt. Meeting her felt like fate. Like it was meant to be. He had no idea what the future held for either of them, but he knew he'd be better off with this girl in his life than without her.

Tex watched as her eyes began to droop. The time between when her eyes were open and when they were closed lengthened, until she was breathing deeply and her hand went limp in his own. And still Tex sat there, unmoving.

It wasn't until a nurse entered that Tex slipped his hand from under Akilah's. He motioned to the nurse that he wanted to talk to her outside.

"She can't understand us, so we can speak freely in here," she said quietly, doing her best not to wake up a sleeping Akilah.

Tex stiffened. "It's not a matter of her not under-standing. It's rude to talk about someone in front of them, *more* so when they can't understand. Now, if you'd please step outside with me?"

He could see she wanted to protest, but she finally nodded and they stepped out into the hall.

"I'm sorry, but who are you to her?" the nurse asked, obviously expecting him to say he was a friend or something.

"I'm her sponsor. Her family. And from this moment on, she's under my protection," he said firmly.

The woman must have seen something in his expression, something that warned her she needed to tread carefully. She nodded.

Tex did his best to sound friendlier as he said, "She's in a bit of pain. She wouldn't admit it, but I could tell. The wound is seeping quite a bit too; the bandage will need to be changed fairly soon, I'd guess." Seeing the woman's confusion at his words, Tex tapped his leg. "Lost a limb myself. I know what to look for."

"Ah. I understand. I'll look at it when I go back in and will check her pain meds."

"Thank you. Oh, and I'll be giving her a phone with an app that translates Arabic to English and English to Arabic. I'd appreciate it if you could spread the word to the staff to have patience with her. It's slow and cumbersome to communicate that way, but she deserves that respect. To be talked to, and not talked *over*. If it's something important, the translator will also be around."

The respect in the woman's eyes increased. "She's a lucky girl."

Tex knew the nurse meant Akilah was lucky because she had *him*, but in reality, she was lucky that she hadn't been killed by the bombs that decimated her village. Lucky that she'd been able to hide from the terrorists who took what they wanted from women without their permission. She was lucky she'd only lost her arm.

"I'll be back this afternoon with my wife, after she's gotten some sleep. I'll leave my number at the nurses' station. I'd appreciate a call immediately if something changes with her situation."

"Yes, sir," the nurse said.

"And the translator will be with her until she's discharged. She'll go home at night, but otherwise, she'll be here making sure Akilah understands everything that's happening around her."

The nurse nodded.

Tex took a deep breath. "I'm sorry if I'm being abrupt. Being in the hospital brings back not-so-good memories for me. I'm also worried about Akilah. Thank you for what you do. I know it's not easy."

The smile that formed on her face was genuine. "We'll take care of her."

"Thank you. I'll be back later," he said, then turned to head down the hall. His mind spun with everything he needed to do. Bringing Akilah home wouldn't be easy, but as the SEAL saying went, "The only easy day was yesterday."

Today was a brand-new day, and he couldn't wait to see what the future held.

———

"Relax, Tex," Melody said softly.

But he couldn't relax. They'd just arrived at the house with Akilah, and he wanted her to like her new home. Her recovery was moving along at a faster-than-expected rate, and her surgeon was pleased that she'd been discharged sooner than everyone had thought she would.

That was all great news, except it meant Tex had to rush to get everything set up for her at home. Akilah had quite a bit of rehab she needed to go through, along with fittings for a prosthetic and practice using it, but Tex could easily help her with all that, since he'd been through it himself. He was more worried about how she'd feel about the house.

She hadn't had a lot of time to deal with what happened to her and her loved ones. A psychologist had met with her a few times, but it would most likely take many more sessions for her to manage her grief, anger, and other feelings about the bombing and her injuries.

For now, Tex just needed to get her inside and

settled, and make sure she was all right with her new home.

Melody and Akilah had bonded completely in the last two weeks. There were times when Tex had walked into the hospital room and found his wife and Akilah laughing hysterically over something or another. Seeing Melody with the girl just reaffirmed what a great mother she'd be.

"Welcome home, Akilah," Melody said as she opened the back door of the car to help her out.

But Tex got there before Melody could, taking Akilah's hand as she swung her legs out. She stood and stared at the house. Tex tried to see it from her eyes and had no idea what she saw. It was a simple house. Nothing too fancy. The neighborhood was middle-class. He led her to the door and opened it.

An excited bark made Tex flinch. He'd forgotten about Baby. About how excited their dog was whenever they came home. It didn't matter if they were gone for five minutes or five hours, Baby always greeted them in the same exuberant way.

"Down, Baby," Tex ordered, and as usual, the hound ignored him.

But to Tex's surprise, she didn't jump up like she sometimes did. Her butt was wagging enthusiastically, but she seemed to understand that Akilah wasn't at one hundred percent. She nuzzled Akilah's hand, begging for pets.

The girl giggled. She went to her knees right there in the foyer and greeted Baby.

Melody sniffed next to him, and Tex had to admit that he felt pretty emotional at the moment himself.

After petting Baby for a while, Akilah fumbled with her pocket and pulled out the phone Tex had gotten for her. He'd downloaded the translation app, and it was one of the best things he could've done for her. Having the freedom to talk to people, and understand what they were saying to her, had brought Akilah out of her shell more than anything else could have. She was still reserved, but didn't look nearly as lost and scared as she had when they'd first met.

"She only has three limbs like us!" Akilah said, the pleasure easy to hear in her tone.

"She lost her leg protecting Tex and me," Melody told her.

Akilah looked down at the dog, who lifted her head and licked her cheek. She giggled again, and Tex closed his eyes at the sound. He felt Melody's arm go around his waist and squeeze, her head resting on his biceps. He was a blessed man.

There was a time when he was a *broken* man. When he thought he might be better off if he'd been killed when he'd lost his leg. But he'd been wrong. His wife and Akilah were proof.

"You want to see your room, Akilah?" Melody asked.

The girl looked up in surprise. "I get a room to myself?" she asked.

Melody smiled. "Yes. Absolutely."

Tex followed the ladies as they headed for Akilah's new bedroom. He had second thoughts about everything he'd done. Wondered if it was too much. If Akilah would be overwhelmed. But it was too late to change anything now.

Melody opened the door and stood back, letting Akilah enter first. She walked inside and looked around with wide eyes. Tex held his breath as he wanted to see what she thought.

There was a double bed against the wall, covered in a pink comforter. Akilah had told Melody during one of her hospital visits that pink was her favorite color. There was also a dresser against one wall, a small desk under the window, pink curtains with big cheery white flowers, and the closet was filled with clothes the girl would probably outgrow before she could wear them all.

But it was the mural on one wall that had Tex feeling as if he might throw up, waiting to see her reaction.

He'd done some research and found out exactly where Akilah had lived. He'd called in a few markers to people he knew in the military, getting satellite pictures of what that part of town had looked like before it was bombed. Then he'd hired an artist to paint a 3D version of one of the streets on the wall. It went from floor to the ceiling, and it was so lifelike, Tex could almost imagine he was standing in Iraq, looking down the street at the homes and businesses on either side.

But would Akilah like it? Or would it make her sad? Tex didn't know...but if she hated it, he had several cans of pink paint in the garage and could have it covered up in a few hours.

The girl stared at the wall without moving. Just when Tex was ready to go to the garage and get the paint, she rushed toward him. She collided with Tex and buried her face in his chest. Her good arm clutched him tightly as she sobbed.

Tex froze in fear. Shit. He'd fucked up. All he'd wanted to do was make her feel more at home. To give her some familiarity in a strange and new world. He hated that he'd made her cry. It was the last thing he wanted to do.

Looking up at him, tears on her cheeks and eyes red, Akilah said in English. "It is home."

Tex was amazed at how fast she was picking up

English. She was by no means fluent, but he had a feeling she understood a lot more than some people thought she did. She was just beginning to use English words when she could, but she was extremely observant and listened to everyone around her.

Tex nodded, the lump in his throat so big, he couldn't speak.

Melody pulled out her phone and clicked the translation app. "Do you like it?" she asked. "Tex wanted to give you something familiar that would make you think of home. If it's too much, we can paint over it."

"No!" Akilah said fiercely as she pulled out of Tex's arms. She walked over to the mural and pointed at a doorway. "My friend Fadila lived here. That store, we bought bread." She put her palm on the wall and closed her eyes.

"Akilah?" Tex asked.

She turned to look at him, and Tex knew in that moment he'd move heaven and earth to give this girl anything she wanted. She had him wrapped around her little finger already, and he didn't even care. "Is it too painful?" he asked, the app translating his words into Arabic. "Don't be afraid to hurt my feelings. Be honest."

Akilah shook her head and walked back to him. She stopped close and said, "It is the most beautiful thing I've ever seen. And the saddest. It is a good reminder for me. Of my family. My friends. But I am glad I am here. In the United States. With you and Melody. And Baby the dog. I like remembering. It makes me feel comfort. Thank you."

"You're welcome, sweetheart," Tex said.

Akilah turned toward the closet and asked, "Who clothes all for?"

Melody laughed. "They're yours, honey."

Akilah's eyes widened. "All me?"

"Yes."

The girl looked around the room once more, taking everything in. Her gaze stopped on the desk. She looked back at Tex. "I can go school?"

"Yes, you'll be going to school," Tex told her.

Once more Akilah's eyes filled with tears. "I didn't go at home. My mother taught me what she could. I supposed to stay home and keep house."

"I'm sorry. I can't tell if you're happy or sad that you'll be going to school," Tex said.

Akilah smiled then. A smile so big, it lit up her whole face. Tex knew he'd never forget this moment. "Happy!" she said.

Tex couldn't stop himself from stepping toward her and hugging her once more. "I'm glad."

Melody joined him, putting her arms around them both. They stood like that for a long moment, enjoying the moment and soaking it in. Then Tex took a deep breath and released his hold on his girls. "How's the arm feeling? I bet it hurts, it's about time for another pill. Why don't you and Mel go and hang out in the living room while I make us a snack?"

"You?" Akilah asked in surprise.

Melody giggled. "Yup. Tex makes the best snacks. Come on, Baby will be thrilled to have another hand to pet her while she sits in your lap."

Tex watched them leave and took a moment to glance around the room. The artist had done a damn good job with the painting, and the fact that Akilah had actually recognized some of the places in the mural was pretty amazing. He knew there would come a time when she no longer needed the familiar sight of her village around her. She'd become more confident and comfortable in her new surroundings. He hoped that she'd decide to stay once she was completely healed.

But no matter what her decision, Tex knew he was blessed to have this time with her. Making a mental note to be sure Doctor Joiner knew how appreciative Tex was of what he'd done, he headed out of the room toward the kitchen. He had some ladies to pamper.

There were several things he needed to do in his basement office. People he needed to check in on.

Intel he needed to research. But for the moment, that could wait. Making sure his new daughter was settling in was more important.

His daughter.

Tex smiled. Some people would think he was crazy for taking on an almost teenager from another country, who couldn't speak English and who'd been through something so traumatic. Not to mention her medical needs and the cost. Tex didn't care. Akilah was meant to be his. And Melody's. No matter if they had babies together in the future or not, Akilah would always be their first child.

He took a moment to enjoy the scene in front of him as he entered the living room. Akilah was sitting on the couch with Baby tucked against her injured side. She was petting her with her hand, the hound's eyes rolled back in her head. She brushed her fingers over the place where Baby's leg should be, then she looked up, catching him staring.

Akilah smiled at him. Tex returned the grin and headed for the kitchen.

Life was full of bumps in the road. Some of those bumps were more like mountainous hills that seemed hard to climb. Followed by dips so deep, they were almost impossible to claw out of. But then the road smoothed out and there were times like this. Times when things were good. Easy. Right.

They wouldn't last. They never did. But with Akilah and Melody at his side, Tex had no doubt they'd make it through any bumps and dips that might happen in the future.

* * *

#TexRocks

If you haven't read Tex's original story, it's called *Protecting Melody*. You'll also find Tex makes an appearance in a LOT of the books in the Operation Alpha fan-fiction world!

Sign up for my newsletter to receive info on all my new releases here:
https://www.stokeraces.com/contact-1.html

SEALING HIS FUTURE

by Susan Stoker

ABOUT THE BOOK

Two of the most popular of Susan Stoker's characters
meet on a Navy SEAL mission...and one finds out the
truth about the woman he thought loved him and
was waiting for him to return home safe and sound.

**This story was originally included in the
Nightingale Charity Anthology which came out in
the summer of 2022 and is no longer available.

SEALING HIS FUTURE

BAKER – 37 years old

Baker Rawlings was tired.

Exhausted.

The last two months had been hell. Of course, when he'd joined the Navy SEALs, he hadn't expected the missions to be sunshine and roses, but for some reason, he hadn't expected every single one to be a nonstop, adrenaline-filled, terror-inducing, this-might-be-my-last-moment-on-earth mission either.

This latest had started out all right. They'd been sent overseas to rescue three prisoners of war. Their intel was solid, and Baker's team was working with another group of SEALs he respected. Their leader was a man named Tex. He was young, but had one of the deepest needs to help others that Baker had ever seen.

The night before everything went to shit, Baker and Tex had gotten a few moments to talk about something other than the battle plan and how they were going to get the three men who'd been taken captive out alive.

They'd spoken about their families, what their first meal would be when they got home from the mission, and whether they had anyone waiting for them back home.

Tex had admitted he didn't have anyone special. Baker had found himself opening up to the young man, telling him about Tabitha.

"I thought she was it for me," Baker said. "That she was the love of my life. But almost as soon as she moved in with me, she changed. Became withdrawn. She seems irritated when I'm home, and just as pissed off when I get orders for a mission. Nothing I do seems to satisfy her."

"So you're breaking up with her when you get back?" Tex asked.

Baker shrugged.

"Look, man. I know I'm younger than you and don't have as much life experience as you, but why are you settling for a woman who doesn't even sound like she likes you all that much?"

Baker shrugged.

"When I get married, it's going to be for good. I'm going to find a woman who loves me exactly how I am, warts and all. She's going to be strong enough to stand on her own two feet when I can't be with her, but still willing to lean on me when shit gets tough. I don't care what she looks like, how much she weighs, or if she already has ten kids when we meet. I just want someone who loves me for me."

Baker snorted and rolled his eyes. "Good luck with that."

"I'm serious," Tex said quietly. "I'd rather be single for the rest of my life than settle for someone who merely tolerates me."

"You gonna make the SEALs a career?" Baker asked. He might think the kid was a little naïve, but he couldn't help but like him all the same.

"Maybe. I'd love to be able to do something with computers. I'm pretty good with them, if I do say so myself. I'd like to use my skills to help the Navy. Find missing people, track down the enemy, use what I know to help soldiers and special forces teams on missions. That kind of thing."

Baker couldn't help but be impressed.

"What about you? You've been doing this SEAL thing for a while now, huh?" Tex asked.

Baker chuckled. "Yeah. I'm a lifer. Not sure what I'll do when I get out. But that time is comin'. Been at this for what seems like all of my adult life."

"Where do you want to go when you're out?" Tex asked.

"Hawaii," Baker said without hesitation. "I want to learn how to surf. Enjoy the warm weather. Eat Hawaiian food."

"Not to mention check out the hot chicks in bikinis," Tex teased.

"Exactly," Baker joked.

Tex stared at him for a long moment before saying, "It's not my place, and we don't even really know each other, but if I've learned anything in my short time as a SEAL, it's to trust my instincts. And if yours are telling you that something's up with the woman who's back at your house, you need to move on."

Baker nodded. "Yeah." He'd pretty much already decided to have a long talk with Tabitha when he got home. Being a SEAL was who he was. If she'd moved in with him hoping he'd quit the military and hang out at home with her, doing a nine-to-five job, she'd seriously misread the situation. He'd loved her once.

And that love had slowly but surely died. It was time for them both to move on.

He hadn't had time to talk to Tex much after that. As team leader, he needed to go over the upcoming mission with his own team. Then they'd had to get some rest before heading out early in the morning to rescue their countrymen.

But as with just about every single mission, nothing had gone right. They'd rescued the POWs, but not before their captors had done their best to take everyone out. Baker's team had sustained several injuries, but thankfully nothing critical.

His new friend Tex, however, had unfortunately stepped in the wrong place at the wrong time and triggered an IED. He was currently being flown to Germany in order to attempt to save at least part of his leg that had been blown to bits...and hopefully his life.

Making friends was a difficult thing in the military. Not only was the government constantly making their soldiers and sailors change duty stations, the risk of losing someone to an explosive, mortar fire, or a stray bullet was extremely high...especially as a SEAL. Baker hadn't met many people he'd had an immediate connection with, but he'd enjoyed spending time with Tex and thought he was uncannily mature for his age. He sent a short prayer into the world for the young man to make it through the many surgeries he'd be undergoing.

Now, it was a relief to finally be heading stateside, although Baker had to deal with Tabitha when he got home. He wanted to hope that things would be different when he got there. That she'd be overjoyed to see him, would sit on the couch and simply hold him while he decompressed. But the chances of that happening were slim to none.

In the last email he'd received from Tabitha, she'd bitched about the lawn work needing to be done, she didn't have enough money to repair her car, and that, when she'd agreed to move in, she hadn't realized she'd be basically living alone.

Sighing, Baker rested his head on the back of his seat on the military plane. He had earphones on, but they weren't plugged in; they were just to keep anyone from attempting to have a long conversation with him. He liked most of the men on his team, but he needed some space.

He thought about the conversation he'd had with Tex once again. How sure the other man had been when he'd talked about finding a woman who loved him exactly how he was. That would be harder with a prosthesis. But he had a feeling if anyone could find someone to love him exactly as is, it would be Tex.

The flight home was long, and Baker should have

slept, but as usual, his mind wouldn't shut down. His time as a SEAL was coming to an end in a few years. He hadn't thought much about what he'd do when he got out...but Tex had inadvertently given him an idea.

Baker also had an affinity for computers. What if he did as Tex suggested? Used his abilities to track down intel? To help the Navy and other governmental agencies get information on men like those they'd just taken out, men who'd taken American soldiers captive?

For the first time in a long time, excitement swam in Baker's veins. He was good at making people trust him. He wanted to combine that with his computer acumen to continue to serve his country, while not having to put himself in the direct line of fire.

But first he needed to deal with Tabitha.

Baker sighed.

The plane touched down, and while he hadn't exactly expected Tabitha to be at the airport to greet him—especially since when the SEALs returned home from a mission, there weren't any big parades or special parties thrown in their honor—he was disappointed nonetheless. Inevitably, there were always a few wives and children waiting. Word would get out, and those who could, always came to meet their loved ones. But not Tabitha.

Baker greeted his team's spouses and made sure

everyone was good to go—and that they'd be at the after-action review of the mission the next afternoon —before heading to his vehicle. He threw his ruck-sack in the backseat before climbing behind the wheel.

It was drizzling, which didn't help his mood. The more he thought about moving to Hawaii once he retired, the more he looked forward to it. Sunshine, cool breezes, and surfing. He needed that more than he'd realized.

Baker pulled into the driveway of his small condo and took a deep breath. The last thing he wanted to do was fight with Tabitha, but he had a feeling what he wanted and what he was going to get were two completely different things.

He hefted his bag over his shoulder and headed up the walk. The condo was quiet and dark. After unlocking the door, Baker walked in and called out, "Tabitha?"

He flicked on the light in the foyer...and winced as he looked around.

Baker wasn't a man who needed a lot of stuff. He didn't especially like clutter, but ever since Tabitha had moved in, his condo had become a dumping ground for all her crap. When he was home, he could keep most of it contained, but in the two months he'd been gone, she'd either been on a ton of shopping sprees, or she'd completely disregarded his need for everything to be in its place.

There were shopping bags all over the couch and table, and clothes were strewn everywhere. Her shoes littered the floor in several places. Baker could just see the counter in the kitchen, and it looked as if there were dirty dishes on every available surface. If she'd done even one load of laundry or dishes in the two months he'd been gone, Baker would be surprised.

The exhaustion that sat heavy on his shoulders pressed down even harder. He wouldn't be able to sleep until at least some of the crap everywhere was cleaned up.

"Tabby!" he bellowed, too angry to walk up the stairs to the bedroom to wake her.

But only silence greeted him.

His head pounding, Baker dropped his rucksack and sighed. He should be worried about where his girlfriend could be, but at the moment, all he could think about was where to start cleaning up the mess she'd left him.

And Tex. He hoped the SEAL was all right. He had no idea if he had family who would head to Germany to sit by his side as he healed. Losing his leg would certainly end his SEAL career, which was a blow to the Navy for sure. Baker had a feeling the man would've risen in the ranks extremely fast.

Just when he was about to head into the kitchen to see the full extent of the damage, and calculate how long it would take him to clean before he could get a shower and some sleep, a knock sounded at the door behind him, making Baker jump.

Laughing a little at himself, he turned and opened it. He blinked in surprise at the police officer standing there.

"Are you Baker Rawlings?" the man asked.

Panic set in. Had something happened to his parents while he'd been deployed? Had Tabitha been in an accident? "Yes," he told the man. "What's wrong? Is it Tabby? Is she okay? Has one of my teammates been injured?"

"No one's been hurt. Can I come in?" the officer asked.

Baker was confused. If no one was hurt, why was the man here? Knowing he wouldn't get any answers until he heard what the officer had to say, Baker backed up and gestured for the man to enter.

"I'd offer you a seat, but as you can see, the place is a mess. I just got home from a mission and I haven't even had a shower yet," Baker said a little grumpily.

"I'm sorry, I won't take much of your time. I'm

Detective Prince. We've been conducting an undercover assignment after receiving a tip. I'm sorry to be the one to tell you this...but Tabitha Grundel has been arrested for conspiracy to commit murder."

Baker blinked. "*Murder*? Who did she want to kill?"

"You."

Baker could only stare at the man. "What?"

"Again, I'm sorry to be the one to break this to you, especially right when you got home. But since getting that tip, we've been following Miss Grundel and her boyfriend. We've had them under constant surveillance. We have hours of phone and text conversations between the two of them and a third person, the one who was actually going to do the deed. The plan was to make it look like a home robbery. Tabitha would have unlocked the back door to your condo to let the third man enter, and when you came downstairs to investigate, he would've shot you. She was then going to call the police and claim someone broke in."

Baker's head was spinning. All he could do was repeat, "*What?*"

"It seems the plan was to collect your life insurance from the Navy and sell all your belongings, then move to California."

"She has a boyfriend?" Baker knew he sounded

completely off-kilter, but he couldn't help it. He needed to think—but right now, it was nearly impossible.

"Yes."

"And he was going to break into my house?"

"Well, not him. But the person they hired to kill you, yes. And technically he wouldn't have had to break in, since Tabitha was going to leave the door open for him."

"Let me guess...she was going to break the window to make it look like that's how he'd gained entry?"

"Yes."

Baker shook his head. He'd known all along Tabby wasn't the smartest person in the world, but she was kind and upbeat, at least in the beginning. She was also beautiful, and pretty decent in bed. Baker was ashamed that he'd let such superficial attributes keep him from seeing the real, apparently *devious* woman underneath.

Then something else the officer said sank in. "Wait—my life insurance?"

"Yes. Apparently she thought that since she was living with you, it would be awarded to her...she mentioned something about being a common-law wife in her texts and conversations with her boyfriend."

"Virginia isn't a common-law state," Baker told the officer, something the man was obviously well aware of.

"You know that, and I know that, but apparently Tabitha and her boyfriend didn't."

Baker rubbed his forehead. His headache had morphed into a full-blown migraine. He should be more upset upon learning his girlfriend had not only been cheating on him, but had plotted to kill him for money that wouldn't ever be hers. Instead, a large part of him was relieved.

He wouldn't have to break up with her. Wouldn't have to deal with telling her that she needed to move out.

"What now?" he asked wearily.

The officer looked sympathetic. "We'd like to have you come down to the station and answer some questions. Give us some background, tell us what you can about Tabitha."

The last thing Baker wanted to do was tell anyone what an idiot he'd been when it came to his now ex-girlfriend. Admit that he'd kept her around longer than he should've simply because it was easier than dealing with her temper and the inevitable outburst that would come with him breaking things off.

"Will the charges stick?" he asked.

"Yes," Detective Prince said firmly. "We waited

until we had all the evidence we needed before arresting her. All three who were involved will see jail time."

Whatever she got wouldn't be enough for Baker, but as of this moment, he didn't care. The moment the detective told him she'd been arrested for conspiring to kill him, he'd already washed his hands of her. She'd have to deal with the consequence of her actions. "I have a meeting on the base I can't get out of tomorrow afternoon. Can I come in the day after tomorrow?"

"Yes, that would be fine. For what it's worth...I'm sorry. This is a pretty crummy thing to come home to after being deployed."

The officer wasn't wrong about that. "Thanks."

"Thank you for your service. I understand you're a Navy SEAL?"

Baker nodded.

"Right. I probably don't need to say this, but... watch your back," Detective Prince said.

Baker straightened. "Do I need to worry about any other players being involved in her plot?" he asked.

"No. But desperate people do desperate things, and Tabitha Grundel was pretty desperate when she was being led away in cuffs. There's no telling what she might do behind bars. Who she might try to contract to finish what she started."

"You *did* tell her that even if I'm dead, she's not getting a penny of my life insurance, right?" Baker asked. "I'm assuming in your reconnaissance and research, you found that my parents are my beneficiaries?"

The officer nodded. "Yes, we did discovered that, and we informed Miss Grundel. But she refused to believe it. She told us that you said you'd take care of her if anything happened to you while you were on a mission."

"Yeah, I would've. My teammates would've made sure she had a place to live and that my final expenses were paid. I didn't mean I was making her my beneficiary," Baker said with a shake of his head.

"Yeah, well, she obviously interpreted that differently," Detective Prince said with a shrug. "Anyway, if you have any questions before we meet, here's my card."

Baker took the business card with a nod. He closed the door behind the man and stared at the wood for a long moment. Then he turned to face the mess that was his house.

Making a split-second decision, Baker headed for the stairs.

Fuck it. He'd clean up later. And by clean up, he

meant throw every single one of Tabitha's belongings into the fucking dumpster.

He made a mental note to talk to his commander tomorrow about transferring to a different base. Maybe across the country, to California. He wanted to check on Tex and make sure he made it through surgery...and look at real estate in Hawaii.

After a long, hot shower, Baker lay on his bed and stared at the ceiling. He was beyond tired, but his mind wouldn't shut down. He thought about what Tex had said, about the kind of woman he was looking for.

"I'm going to find a woman who loves me exactly how I am, warts and all. She's going to be strong enough to stand on her own two feet when I can't be with her, but still willing to lean on me when shit gets tough. I don't care what she looks like, how much she weighs, or if she already has ten kids when we meet. I just want someone who loves me for me."

Baker wanted that. The problem was, he wasn't sure she existed. He was almost forty, and if he hadn't found his other half by now, he was afraid he never would. All his life, he'd felt as if she was out there... somewhere. But finding her had turned out to be more difficult than he'd ever expected.

He'd once thought Tabitha was that woman, the other half of his soul, but even before he'd asked her to move in, he realized she wasn't. Rather than be lonely, he'd continued to date her anyway.

No more. Baker was done with casual dating. It didn't matter if he never had sex again; he wouldn't settle for another half-assed relationship. He'd rather be celibate and alone the rest of his life than be tied to someone he wasn't madly and passionately in love with.

He wanted someone who made him laugh. Who didn't mind his protective personality. Who could stand at his side and be proud of him, and who was strong enough to withstand anything life might throw their way. He wanted someone selfless and friendly, who would be happy to see him again whether they were apart two hours or two months.

In return, she'd get all of him. Everything that he was. His devotion, his loyalty, and he'd do whatever it took to protect her from the shit life had a way of throwing at people. If she was out there, she'd be the most important person in his life, and he'd make sure she knew that with every fiber of her being.

Baker sighed.

He was being maudlin. He wasn't sure such a woman existed. At least not for him.

He had a few more years of service in the Navy to go, but then he was retiring, moving to Hawaii and becoming a beach bum. He would see about using his skills to continue to serve his country. He'd stay busy and single...and that would have to be enough.

Just as he drifted off to asleep, he had a hazy vision of a woman with brown hair, wrinkles around her eyes, and a laugh that made everyone around them turn and stare. She was petite, with more pain in her gaze than any one person should have to bear.

And when she turned to look at him, she whispered, "Be patient, Baker. Our time will come."

* * *

If you've read any of my stories, you've met Tex and know he didn't let losing his leg hold him back. He's been an anchor for so many of my Heroes and heroines. I loved connecting Tex with BAKER. If you want to know more about the mysterious Baker, you can start with *Finding Elodie*, which is the first book in my SEAL Team Hawaii Series. His story will come...

Read on!

FINDING PEYTON

by Susan Stoker

In the Summer of 2022, I was invited by the amazing Lucy Score to go into her reader group on Facebook and participate in a thing she calls "Tell Me A Story."
And I said yes! ha.
I went in one night and posted some polls about the to-be-written story. What the name of the heroine should be, the nickname of the Hero, and other facts.
There was also a "wild card" question where her readers could give me all sorts of crazy things that I would have to incorporate into the story. I picked a few and sat down and wrote.
This is the story that I came up with.
I loosely tied it to my Hawaii SEAL series and of

course had to include both Tex and Baker...
because...why not?
I hope they enjoyed it, and now I'm sharing it with
you and I hope you all enjoy it too!
~Susan

ABOUT THE BOOK:
When Peyton realizes she's purposely been left in the
middle of the ocean to die, she almost panics...until
she realizes that the handsome Navy SEAL she'd
been ogling earlier on the boat that had ditched
them, had been left behind as well.

FINDING PEYTON

PEYTON HULSEMAN LIFTED her head and took the snorkel out of her mouth and took a deep breath. As much as she loved snorkeling, she didn't love clenching the plastic in her mouth and breathing through a tube. She'd been following a sea turtle and had been enchanted and awed by its movements and how it didn't even seem to notice her following it.

She'd decided to go ahead and go on this vacation by herself at the last minute. She and her boyfriend, now only to be known as Douchecanoe, had broken up two months earlier. They'd planned this vacation in better times, obviously, and for some insane reason, he'd thought she would cancel their reservations and give him half the money. Which was ridiculous because he hadn't paid for anything in the first place. Not the airplane tickets. Not the hotel. Not the cost of the excursions they'd planned.

When she'd finally realized what a mooch, and money-grubbing jerkface he was, Peyton had been embarrassed. He'd apparently only been with her because of the size of her bank account...which was considerable. Her family owned a very successful business and the money she brought in with her own job wasn't anything to sneeze at.

She was going to cancel the trip to Oahu— because who went on vacation by themselves, to Hawaii of all places—but her best friend, Marley, talked her into going anyway. And now, after following that turtle for what seemed like miles, but probably was only a couple hundred yards or so, she was even more thankful she'd gone outside her comfort zone and come to Hawaii by herself.

Blinking water out of her eyes, Peyton looked around for the boat. She was thirsty and tired and could really go for one of the tacos the captain had promised he'd have ready for her when she got out of the water. But to her surprise, she saw nothing but water all around her.

Frowning, she turned in the other direction, only to see the outline of Diamond Head, what she thought was the old extinct volcano on the coast of Oahu in the distance, the very, *very* far distance.

"Oh shit," she mumbled disbelievingly.

She'd missed the boat. Or it had left without her.

Either way she was screwed.

Peyton wanted to laugh. This was completely typical of something that would happen to her. She was constantly late to things back home in Oregon. Marley was constantly bitching about her showing up ten, twenty, even sometimes an hour or more late to outings. It wasn't that Peyton wanted to be late, she just got caught up in her work and lost track of time. The same as she'd done with that turtle.

Surprisingly, she wasn't freaking out though. She didn't know why, maybe because she was already thinking up how to use this ridiculous situation in one of her upcoming cartoons. Drawing was how she dealt with things in her life. When she was sad, that tended to come out in her characters. If someone pissed her off, they'd show up in a cartoon doing something stupid or embarrassing. It was cathartic for her, and being left in the middle of the ocean during a snorkeling excursion was definitely something that needed to be immortalized in a cartoon.

A sound behind her had Peyton shrieking in fright and spinning around. She imagined a huge blue whale lunging at her with its mouth open ready to swallow her down. Or a Great White shark coming at her. Or the turtle she'd been distracted by laughing at her predicament.

For a moment, Peyton seriously thought she was having a heart attack and was about to come face-to-face with a sea monster from the deep. A black head appeared with huge bug eyes. It took a moment for her brain to understand what she was seeing. It wasn't a sea creature, but a man. A very specific man at that.

Relief swam through Peyton's veins. The first thought was that she wasn't alone. The second, was... oh crap.

The man lifted his facemask and took the scuba mouthpiece off his mouth. His brow was furrowed, and his lips drawn down in a frown. But even with that foreboding look on his face, the man was gorgeous.

When he'd first walked up to the boat she'd already boarded and informed her, and the captain, that he was there for the scuba trip, it had been all she could do not to drool. He was taller than her five foot eight by at least half a foot. Muscular, short dark hair, thick thighs, arms that barely fit into the T-shirt he was wearing, and the icing on the cake were the tattoos she could see on one of his calves and on his upper arm.

He was utterly beautiful, and for a second, Peyton was lost in a daydream where he'd take one look at her and fall madly in love and they'd run off and get married and have beautiful babies together. Then she'd snorted, and he'd looked at her in surprise, and all her dreams died.

Why would this man look twice at her? She had frizzy hair, carried too much weight to be considered pretty by society's standards, was an extreme introvert, and tended to say the most inappropriate things at the worst times. And...she snort laughed.

"Where's the boat?" the man, who'd introduced himself as Rob, asked gruffly from the water next to her, bringing her back to the present with a jolt.

Peyton snort laughed. "Gone," she said with a small shrug.

"Shit."

She couldn't help it, Peyton laughed again.

"I'm not sure this is funny," Rob told her, arching a brow in her direction.

"It's not," Peyton told him. "But then again, it kind of is. I mean, think about it. What are the odds?"

To her surprise, Rob actually seemed to be considering the question. "I should've seen this coming," he said after a moment.

Peyton was intrigued. "Why? Can you see the future? Can you read minds?"

Rob chuckled and as inappropriate as it was,

Peyton felt her nipples harden. How in the world could she think about anything other than how they were going to get back to land?

"My ex wasn't happy that I decided to go on this trip without her."

Peyton's eyes widened. "You too?" she blurted.

He stared at her as if she was the only person on the planet. As if they weren't treading water in the middle of the ocean and would probably die out there if the captain didn't realize he was missing two of his guests and came back for them.

"Yeah," Rob said after a moment.

"Wow. That's a coincidence," Peyton said with a shrug.

"When Bertie and I broke up she wanted me to transfer the reservations into her name so she could come out here with some of her friends," Rob said.

"Douchecanoe wanted me to give his half of the money spent on this trip, except he didn't pay for any of it," Peyton admitted.

Rob's lips twitched. "When I told Bertie I wouldn't do it and I was actually going to go to Hawaii without her, I swear I saw fire shoot out of the top of her head."

"When I depicted Douchecanoe as a money grubbing asshat in one of my cartoons, he threatened to sue me for defamation, even though I hadn't used his name and there was no resemblance to him whatsoever."

Rob's head tilted and Peyton swore he'd swooshed himself closer to where she was treading water. "Cartoons?"

Peyton was proud of her little comic strip. She worked hard to come up with funny and creative storylines each week, and was paid extremely well for what she did. But it was still hard to believe her penchant for doodling had led to an actual career. That she was paid money for doing what she loved. "Yeah. I have a weekly comic strip that's published online on about a hundred and forty different websites. I just signed a contract for someone to turn my drawings into live action clips for TikTok and the first one went up a week or so ago and already has two million views." She wasn't bragging, not really. It was still a little unbelievable, but she proud and thrilled that she could entertain people with her drawings.

"What's it called?"

"Should we be trying to figure out how to get back to land?" she asked.

"Probably," Rob said, staring at her expectedly.

His attention was heady. Most people looked past her when they bothered to look at her at all. She wasn't exactly tall, blonde, and stacked. Having this man's complete attention was making her tingle in places she hadn't tingled in a very long time.

"I'm sure you haven't heard of it."

"Humor me," he ordered.

And there was no mistaking that his words were an order. For a split-second Peyton wondered what he'd do if she refused. But decided not to push him. "Pecky the Traveling Taco," she told him almost defiantly.

She'd had every reaction under the sun when she told people what the name of her comic strip was. Laughter, disbelief, eye rolls, condescending remarks...you name it, she'd experienced it. So she was ready for just about anything from Rob, except what she got.

"Are you kidding me? You're fucking with me, aren't you?" he asked with wide eyes.

"Nope. I know it's silly, but tacos are one of my favorite foods, and I was eleven and eating out with my grandparents one day. They took me to this hole-in-the-wall taco place near their house and I got lost in my head imagining my taco standing up and walking around the room and deciding he wanted to go on an adventure and meet people." Peyton pressed her lips together. Shoot, she hadn't meant to admit that. Usually when she told others how she came up with the name and idea for her comic she kept things vague. But for some reason, maybe it was the situation, she'd gone and told Rob the real story.

"That is one of my favorite comics. My friends and I talk about it all the time."

Peyton rolled her eyes. "Whatever," she said, turning her head and looking in the direction of the mainland. She hated when people were condescending about her work. It might be "only" a comic strip, but she loved what she did.

"My favorite is the one where Pecky and his friend, Torty the tortilla decide to go to an amusement park, and while they're on a roller coaster his lettuce comes out and sprays all the people in the cars behind them and they have to get the park employees to find all his missing parts and everyone screams when they see him 'naked'," Rob told her.

Peyton turned back to him with wide eyes. "You've seen my stuff," she said in awe.

"Seen and loved," Rob reassured her.

Then he surprised her by lifting his hand out of the water and holding it out to her. "I'm Rob. Rob Welch. My friends call me Snacker."

Automatically, Peyton reached for his hand. She grabbed hold and said, "I'm Peyton. Peyton Hulseman. My friends call me Peyton."

Rob smiled at her and the feel of his hand in hers

made sparks shoot from her fingertips to her toes... and everywhere in between.

To her shock, he pulled on her hand until they were almost touching chest to chest. Her flipper covered feet brushed against his. "Are you okay?" he asked seriously.

Peyton frowned. "Yes. Why? Are you?"

"I'm good. But you aren't freaking out."

"Would it do any good?" she asked seriously.

"Well, no, but that doesn't usually seem to matter in cases like this."

"You find yourself marooned in the middle of the ocean a lot?" she quipped.

His lips twitched again. She actually wasn't trying to be funny, but if he thought she was, she'd take it.

"Honestly? Not this exact situation, but ones like it, yes."

Peyton couldn't help but be intrigued. "Yeah?"

Rob sighed. "I'm a Navy SEAL."

"Of course you are," she said with a roll of her eyes. She was very aware that he hadn't let go of her hand, but she was in no hurry to let go of him. The truth was the longer they were out here, the more worried she was getting. She was a good swimmer, but there was no way she could swim all the way back to the island.

"I am," Rob insisted. "I'm on leave at the

moment, as you already know, this vaca had already been planned and my commander and team insisted I go. You know, to relax."

She chuckled. "And here you are...relaxing."

He returned her grin. "Or something like that. Anyway, I've participated in my fair share of jungle rescues, kidnapping extractions, not to mention covert operations all over the world. So trust me when I tell you that you aren't reacting like most people who found themselves in your situation would."

Peyton sighed. "I know, I'm weird." She'd been described that way more than once in her lifetime.

"No, you're perfect," Rob said gently.

* * *

Rob stared at the woman bobbing in the waves in front of him. When he'd first caught sight of her on the very boat he was about to board, everything within him had sat up and taken notice. He'd vowed to stay away from women for the foreseeable future after things with Bertie had gone so wrong. He was done with psycho girlfriends, with women trying to manipulate him, with being with chicks who just wanted to bone a Navy SEAL.

But then he'd seen Peyton. Her frizzy red hair was out of control, her clothes were too big and not fashionable in the least, and she didn't look as if she gave a single little shit what anyone else thought about her. He loved that.

To his delight they were the only two customers on board, and Rob looked forward to getting to know the intriguing woman, his vow to keep far away from women long forgotten. But somehow he'd gotten into a conversation with the captain about sea currents and the fishing conditions and hadn't had a chance to even talk to her before they'd arrived at the spot the captain thought would be perfect for snorkeling and scuba diving.

When he'd surfaced and hadn't seen any sign of the boat, he'd immediately known what had happened. Bertie had threatened that if he went to Hawaii without her, she'd make him sorry. Somehow, she'd arranged for him to get left out here in the middle of the ocean. He supposed she thought this was a perfect punishment for a SEAL, for a man who was perfectly comfortable in the water. It wasn't fair that Peyton had gotten dragged into her nefarious plot as well.

But she was taking things amazingly well. He'd

been attracted to her before, but now that he knew she wasn't one to be hysterical when things didn't go her way, *and* that she was the brilliant artist and brains behind Pecky and the Traveling Taco, the cartoon he and his teammates loved to talk about, he was a goner.

"I'm not perfect," she snorted in response to his earlier comment.

He was still holding her hand, and Rob was thrilled beyond belief she hadn't let go.

"Prove it," he challenged.

"What?"

"Prove it," he repeated. "Tell me something about you that isn't perfect."

"Ha, how long do you have?" she retorted.

Pretending to look around, Rob shrugged. "I'm thinking we have some time."

"Shouldn't we be doing something? I don't know, like swimming toward shore or something?" she asked.

"Can you swim the eleven miles, give or take, to Oahu?" he asked.

"Can *you*?" she immediately returned.

"Yes," he said without hesitation.

"Of course you can," she mumbled.

"Come on, Peyton, tell me something you think

isn't perfect about yourself. We'll take turns sharing info."

"Fine. My grandmother can fart on command. She takes great pride in farting in the most inappropriate times."

Rob burst out laughing. "Seriously?"

"Yup," Peyton said with a grin. "Your turn. Why is your nickname Snacker?"

"Because I love junk food."

"What's your favorite?"

"That's like asking a Lucy Score fan what their favorite book of hers is."

Peyton's eyes got huge in her face. "You know who Lucy Score is?"

"Yup. I've even read some of her books."

"You're lying."

"Nope."

"Are you gay?"

Rob laughed. "No. Not even close. I had a girl-friend once who read romance. A lot of it. And I got curious and when she was at work I started to read one of her books. It was eye-opening. Like I'd found the holy grail in how women think and what they want in a guy."

"Wow. I'm gobsmacked."

Rob grinned. He loved being able to shock this woman.

"And don't think I didn't catch that you didn't answer my question," Peyton said.

"About my favorite snack? I like everything. Little Debbies, candy, chocolate, cake, cookies, potato chips, Fritos, funyons, but I do have one weakness…" He let his voice trail off.

"What?"

"Nope, your turn again."

Peyton let out an adorable disgruntled huff of breath. "Fine. My neighbor back in Oregon has a goat named Oreo. He escaped one day and it took two weeks for anyone to catch him. I think he had the time of his life."

"You wrote about that in one of your comic strips," Rob said.

"Yeah. It was hilarious and I was rooting for Oreo for sure."

"That's awesome, although that's not really a fact about you, so I'm not sure that counts."

"Sure it is…I told you I was from Oregon," Peyton said with a smirk.

"Right. I'm currently stationed in Southern California. In a town called Riverton. It's basically San Diego. It's not too far from Oregon." Rob knew he was being as transparent as a piece of glass, but he was thrilled they didn't live on opposite sides of the country. It would make seeing her again much easier.

"I've been there," she told him. "It was a cute town."

"It is," Rob agreed. He felt completely out of his element. He should be thinking of a plan to get them back to the mainland. But holding this woman's hand, treading water, and getting to know her was more important at the moment.

"So...your favorite snack?" she probed.

"Thin mints," he said with a shrug.

"Really? Aren't they seasonal?"

"For most people yes. But back home, when I'm there, I volunteer with a Girl Scout Troop. I teach them things like tying knots, boating, safe water practices, and I take them camping...in return, I get paid in cookies." He grinned at the surprised look on Peyton's face.

"I bet you're great with them," she said in a sincere voice.

"They're awesome," Rob said with a shrug. "They have an unending well of curiosity, and it's fun to see them get excited about the things I'm teaching them."

"I've never been camping," Peyton blurted.

"I'm sorry," Rob said.

Peyton shrugged. "My parents are rich. That's not usually something I tell men I've just met, but I'm thinking this situation isn't exactly normal. We didn't spend time camping or getting dirty when I was growing up...much to my grandmother's dismay. She always told my parents that I should be running around like a heathen getting into trouble and playing in the dirt. But they disagreed."

"Your grandmother was right."

"Well, she also likes to go to drag queen shows on the weekends, so I'm thinking my parents might have had a reason to dismiss her thoughts."

Rob burst out laughing. "I want to meet this grandma of yours," he blurted.

"She'd love you," Peyton told him with a smile. "Your turn."

Rob wracked his brain to think of what else he could tell her about himself. "I'm allergic to seafood," he said with a shrug. It wasn't a terribly exciting fact, but it was all he could think of at the moment.

Peyton stared at him for a minute, then chuckled.

"What?"

"It's just...here you are...surrounded by water... The only thing around in miles to eat is seafood...and you can't eat it."

"We aren't going to have to eat fish or any other creature swimming around us."

Peyton frowned. "You don't know that. And I'm not exactly ready to give up and die."

"We aren't dying," Rob reassured her.

She tilted her head and stared at him for a beat. "What aren't you telling me? What do you know?"

Rob shrugged. "You'll think it's creepy," he said.

"If it's something that will get us out of this water, put a taco in my hand, and put me on dry land in a bed, I'm not going to think it's creepy."

The only thing Rob could think about was her lying on a bed...preferably with him. But now wasn't the time or place for that kind of thinking. "Right, so I'm a Navy SEAL. I have friends with connections. One in particular is a former SEAL who has taken it upon himself to keep others safe. He'd a one-man stalker...and I mean that in a good way. He's made these tracker things. My team wears them when we're on a mission. It's comforting to know if we're ever taken prisoner, this former SEAL will know where we are and will send in the calvary to get us out. This wet suit I'm wearing...it's the one I wear when I'm on a mission. I forgot that I still had one of those trackers in the pocket. I activated it when I realized we'd been left."

"Wait, wait, wait, are you telling me that there's a guy out there somewhere..." she gestured toward Oahu with the hand that wasn't in Rob's... "will see that you're floating out here in the ocean and will notify someone to come get you?"

"That's what I'm hoping," Rob told her.

"How will he know it's you? That you're not out here on a boat or something? Who will he contact? Will he come himself?"

Rob chuckled at the rapid-fire spate of questions. "Each tracker has its own code, the one I have is associated with a number that is uniquely mine. He might think I'm on a boat, but he'll also ask questions to make sure, that's what he does. He's got contacts on Oahu that I'm sure he'll reach out to, and no, he won't come himself."

"Someone's going to come get us?" Peyton asked quietly.

"Yes," Rob said with conviction.

Peyton closed her eyes and for the first time Rob could see how stressed she really was. Her jokes and the back-and-forth info gathering was a way for her to cope. He frowned, making a mental note to look beyond her bubbly personality in the future. To make sure he helped her deal with stress and that she wasn't hiding it from him.

He wasn't even freaked out about the "in the future" thing. This woman was meant to be his. He knew it down to the marrow of his bones. He just had to convince her of that.

"We just have to stay relaxed. They'll come for us," he said fervently.

Peyton's eyes opened and she met his gaze. Her

hazel eyes swam with tears as she nodded. She'd hidden her trepidation a little too well for Rob's liking. He pulled on her hand without thought, and wrapped his free arm around her, holding her against his chest.

It didn't take much to keep them afloat, he'd always been extremely buoyant and the salt water helped even more. Peyton buried her head against his neck and held on tightly. He had the sudden urge to feel her against him without their wetsuits between them. To feel her curves against his body as they lay together in bed after making love.

"I'm sorry," she mumbled against him.

"About what?" he asked.

"For putting you in this situation."

Her words surprised Rob. He pulled back, to try to look into her eyes, but didn't let go of her. But Peyton refused to look up at him.

"What are you talking about?" he asked.

He felt more than heard her sigh as they bobbed in the gentle waves.

"Douchecanoe did this. I know he did."

"Did what?" Rob asked.

"Arranged for me to get left out here in the middle of the ocean. He swore I'd regret not giving him his half of the money this trip cost...even though he wasn't his money. We'd pre-planned this excursion and somehow he convinced the captain to leave me. You just got caught in his evil plan."

"Bertie threatened me too," Rob told her. "She knew my plans as well. Knew I wanted to go scuba diving while I was here. She didn't understand it, saying I spent so much time in the water as it was, why would I want to spend my vacation doing the same thing I do when I'm working. But this is nothing like work. I can take my time and look at the wildlife and plants and stuff. When I'm on a mission, that's the last thing I'm thinking about. It could've just as easily been her who set this up and you were caught in *her* evil plan."

Peyton looked up at him then. "Why are people so...horrible?" she whispered.

"I don't know."

"Well, Bertie might hate you, which is ridiculous —how could someone hate someone with a butt as nice as the one you have?— but my ex thinks he'll get millions of dollars if I end up dead."

Her compliment felt good, but it was the last part of what she said that had him blinking in disbelief. "What?"

"My parents are Claire and Fernando Crown. They started their own company when they were in their twenties. They were bought out a few years ago by a huge manufacturer in a five hundred-million-dollar deal. And that was a low-bid."

Peyton was staring at him as if she was waiting for him to grow two heads and turn into some sort of sea monster. "Good for them," he said after a beat.

Her lips twitched. "You have no idea who they are, do you?"

"Nope."

"Crown Condoms," she said matter-of-factly.

Realization dawned. "Wow," he said.

"Yeah."

"So...you're a condom princess. Cool."

She snort laughed again, and Rob couldn't help but think it was the most adorable sound he'd ever heard.

"That's all you're gonna say? Rob, I'm the heir to a condom dynasty. I'm worth millions. I mean, millions. Plural times a gazillion."

"And Douchecanoe thinks he's gonna get that money?" Rob asked.

Peyton shrugged. "There was a time when I thought we'd get married that we talked about me putting him as my beneficiary. I think he was conceited enough to think I'd already done it. For the record...I didn't."

"Right. Well, when we get rescued, we'll figure it out. Right about now it doesn't matter if it was your ex or mine or orchestrated this little adventure. All that matters is us keeping calm until the Hawaii Navy SEALs arrive."

"You're not what I expected when I first saw you," Peyton blurted.

Rob grinned. "I like keeping you on your toes."

"Or flippers," Peyton said.

"That too."

"This is *so* going in a comic," she informed him.

Rob sighed dramatically. "My teammates are gonna be so jealous that I'm in a Pecky the Traveling Taco cartoon. I'm going to rub it in their faces all the damn time."

His heart swelled in his chest as Peyton lowered her head back to his shoulder and clung to him a little tighter. He held her against his body and couldn't help but sigh in contentment. This situation could've been a hundred times worse than it was. The weather could've been crap, Peyton could've been a complete bitch and a pain in his ass, and he could've decided to rent a wetsuit instead of use his own.

He had no doubt someone would be coming for them. Tex would come through, he had no doubts whatsoever.

* * *

. . .

Peyton had no idea how long they'd been bobbing in the ocean, but she was getting tired. And extremely thirsty. And a little nauseous. She'd wanted to ditch her facemask and snorkel, but Rob insisted on her keeping it...just in case.

It was that 'just in case' that was making her uneasy right about now. The only thing keeping her from freaking out was how calm Rob was. How sure he was that someone would be coming to get them. The sun was beginning to set and the thought of being out here in the dark wasn't a pleasant one. She'd never been afraid of sharks and other marine animals before, but this situation was changing her mind.

She'd never been a clingy type of woman, but she couldn't seem to let go of Rob. His arms felt so warm and right around her, and he'd proven more than able to keep them both afloat.

They'd talked about everything from their favorite books, to food they liked, to more serious things like their political leanings, terrorism, and the state of the world in general. He was funny, but could be serious and deep at the same time. She'd learned about some of his teammates and had told him more stories about her eccentric grandmother and family.

"Hear that?" he asked suddenly.

Jerking in his arms, because she'd actually been on the verge of falling asleep, Peyton lifted her head. She followed his gaze to the horizon and saw what she thought was a boat coming straight for them.

"Holy crap, you were right!" she exclaimed.

"You doubted me?" Rob teased?

She had, but was too ashamed to admit it. "Of course not. You're one of the few and the proud."

He chuckled. "That's the marines, honey."

"Right, sorry. "Army Strong?"

"Peyton," he warned.

She giggled.

"Oh, I know, Born Ready."

"How the hell do you know all the military slogans?" he asked with a shake of his head and a grin on his lips.

"Love me a man in uniform," she quipped.

"The only easy day was yesterday," he informed her. "That's the SEAL Motto."

"Well, they aren't wrong," she said dryly. "Yesterday I was sitting on the beach with a drink in my hand and my tablet in my lap drawing Pecky sitting on a beach with a drink in *his* hand."

She smiled at Rob, but saw that he wasn't even listening to her. His eyes were glued on the horizon and he was frowning. "Rob?" she asked nervously.

He turned his head to her and the intensity of his gaze made her suck in a breath. "Don't panic," he said firmly.

"You know saying that makes me *want* to panic, right?" she asked.

"I'm not sure the boat coming toward us is my friends."

"How can you tell? I mean, it's too far away for me to see much of anything."

"I just do. I need you to trust me."

"I do," Peyton said immediately without thought. It was weird, but she totally trusted this man. If she'd been stuck out here on her own, she would've been in a heap of trouble. But having him here to talk to, his calm demeanor, his belief that his friend would track him and send help, had been a lifeline.

"We need to go under the water. If this is my friends, they'll stop right where we are because they'll have the tracker info. If it's not, they'll go by and we'll know."

Peyton saw his lips say the words, heard them, but they didn't make sense. "I'm not sure how long I can hold my breath," she whispered.

"We'll share my air," he said as if he was informing them that they were going to go for an after-dinner walk on the sand.

"I don't know—"

"I'm not going to let anything happen to you. You know why?"

Glancing at the boat which was still heading for them at breakneck speed, Peyton found she was having a hard time breathing.

Then Rob's finger touched her chin and gently forced her to look into his eyes. "You know why?" he repeated.

Peyton shook her head.

"Because I want to meet your grandmother. I want to thank your parents for starting their condom company because I've used Crown condoms many times over the years. I want to share my thin mints with you and introduce you to my Girl Scouts. I want to meet Oreo, and watch you draw your Pecky cartoons. I want a future. With you, Peyton. And I can't have that if I don't keep you safe right now. Understand?"

Peyton couldn't look away from Rob if someone paid her. She wanted all that too. Desperately. This was the craziest meet-cute ever. No romance novelist would ever write about this because it was so unbelievable. And yet, here she was. Head over heels in love with a Navy SEAL who'd just said they had to go underwater to be safe and he'd share his tank of air with her. All she could do was nod.

"Good." Then Rob shocked the shit out of her by

dropping his head. He covered her lips with his own and even though the odds of them getting away from whoever was determined to see them dead weren't great, her nipples hardened and her inner core tightened. The kiss was rough, and desperate on both their parts. When he lifted his head, his pupils were dilated and he was breathing hard for the first time since she'd met him.

"I want you, Peyton Hulseman. In my bed, in my shower, in my life, my ring on your finger, and my baby in your belly."

Holy shit. This man was intense. And Peyton was there for it.

"Yes," she said simply.

He grinned. The intense scary look disappeared from his face as if they were the only two people on earth in a tropical paradise instead of about to be run over by a boat going way too fast toward them.

"Right. Take a deep breath, sweetheart, and put your mask down. We're going under. We'll pass my regulator back and forth and take turns breathing. I've got you."

Peyton nodded, although she definitely wasn't sure about this.

Rob fiddled with something on the vest he was wearing pulled down his own mask, and way before she was ready, they began to sink under the surface.

Luckily, she'd taken a breath when he'd told her to. Even as they sunk below the waves, he held his out mouthpiece to her. For a second she didn't think she'd be able to get her body to obey what she was telling it to do. Breathing in while underwater wasn't natural, even with the regulator in her mouth. But then Rob squeezed her waist, he hadn't let go of her even for a second, and she forced herself to relax.

She nodded at Rob and he brought the mouth-piece to his own face and took a breath. They took turns, breathing in the oxygen and the sound of something over their heads caught her attention. Looking up, Peyton saw a boat zip over their heads, going just as fast as it had when she'd first seen it.

So Rob had been right. These weren't his friends. It wasn't someone coming to rescue them. It was probably whoever had left them out here in the first place, wanting to make sure they were dead. The thought made her shiver, and Rob's arm tightened around her once more. Reassuring her. Keeping her calm.

How long they stayed under the water taking turns breathing the oxygen in the tank on Rob's back, Peyton didn't know. But when he tapped her shoulder and pointed up, she wasn't sure she wanted to surface just yet. If whoever had come back for them was still up there, he could see them and finish what he'd started. She shook her head.

Rob palmed her cheek and stared at her through his facemask. He wasn't rushing her, would give her all the time she needed...well, all the time they had left in the oxygen tank that is. She wasn't stupid, knew they had to be getting low. But the patience Rob showed gave her the bravery she needed to nod. Without hesitation, Rob turned a knob on his vest and air bubbles burst forth and headed for the surface, just as they did.

They floated up and Peyton looked around frantically as their heads broke the surface of the waves. She saw nothing. No boat.

Rob didn't hesitate to push the mask off her face to the top of her head. He gently took the mouthpiece out of her mouth, then pushed his own mask up. Then he took her face in his hands and pulled her roughly into him. She let out an *oof* as she made contact with his chest, but then his lips were once more on hers.

And this time Peyton didn't hold back. She kissed him back as hard as she could. Showing him without words how much he was beginning to mean to her. How grateful she was he was there. How much she admired him.

Their lips twined together, just as their legs did.

She frantically wrapped her arms around his back, trying to get closer.

"Easy, sweetheart, you're okay," Rob crooned.

It wasn't until she heard him speak that Peyton realized she was breathing way too fast. Almost hyperventilating.

"They're gone. You're okay."

"I can't believe we just did that," she panted against his neck as she held onto him as tightly as she could.

"Kiss?"

She huffed out a breath. "No. *That* was awesome. Stupendous. Amazing. I mean sharing your air thing."

"You were amazing. Are you sure you haven't done that before?" he joked.

Peyton pulled back. "Not even close," she said.

At her tone, his smile died. "I mean it," he told her in a serious tone. "I can count on one hand the number of people I'd trust to do that with."

"Will they be back?" she whispered, talking about whoever was in the boat.

"No."

Frowning, she said, "You don't know that."

"Then why'd you ask me?"

"I don't know."

"They aren't coming back. They came out to make sure we were well and truly gone so they could report back to either Douchecanoe or Bertie. The next people we see will be my Navy SEAL friends. I give you my word."

"Okay," Peyton whispered.

"Okay," he echoed. Then added, "I was serious, you know."

"About what?"

"About wanting to be with you once we get on dry land."

"Your hotel or mine?" she quipped.

"Don't care. But I want more than that, Peyton. Riverton isn't Oregon, I know that, and I can't change where I'm stationed, but I'll do whatever it takes to make you happy. I'll come up every weekend. I have lots of leave saved up, I don't take many vacations, so I can visit as often as you'll have me. I want to introduce you to my team and show you Riverton. There are lots of SEAL wives there who I think you'd really love. My mentor's wife, Caroline, is a lot like you. Smart as hell, a little introverted, but as sweet as she could be. And Wolf couldn't love her more."

He was talking fast, too fast for Peyton to be able to get a word in.

"And you can come camping with me and my Girl Scouts. I can probably put in a good word for you and get you in the Thin Mint supply line if you wanted.

Anything you want, I'll bend over backward to make happen. Just please tell me you'll give me a chance."

When he paused to breathe, Peyton asked, "You done?"

"Um...maybe?" he said a little sheepishly.

"You know my job can be done from anywhere," she said a little shyly. She couldn't believe she was saying this, much less even thinking it. "I mean, have tablet, will travel. I could draw Pecky from Riverton as well as I could from Oregon."

Rob's eyes opened wide, then he said, "Yes!"

Peyton smiled.

"My apartment isn't super grand, but I can look for a bigger one. We can find one with an office, maybe with a view of the beach, so you can have some inspiration when you draw. I can't wait to see Pecky discover Riverton!"

It was insane that they were discussing moving in together when they'd known each other for...hell, she had no idea how long it had been, but she didn't care. This felt right. More right than anything she'd ever done in her life. "My grandma is going to love you," she whispered. "She's always loved a man in uniform too. Her favorite drag shows are the ones where they dress like pin-ups from the fourties."

Rob grinned. "How'd I get so lucky?"

Peyton couldn't hold back the snort-laugh.

"Lucky? Rob, we're still stranded in the middle of the ocean, in case you've forgotten."

"I haven't forgotten. But my SEAL friends will be here in less than five minutes and we'll have blankets, water, food, and soon I'll get you in my bed. How could I be anything but lucky?"

Alarmed, Peyton looked toward the mainland and saw another boat headed in their direction. She inhaled sharply.

"Relax. That's the Navy," Rob said completely calmly.

"How do you know? It could be that other boat coming back!" she exclaimed.

"I can tell by the motor. It's the Navy," he said firmly.

Peyton looked at the man she was still holding onto almost desperately. "Are you sure?"

"I'm sure."

Taking a deep breath, Peyton nodded. "It's almost over."

"No, it's only the beginning," he countered.

"Are you always this...pragmatic?" she asked. "Because I have to say...it could get annoying."

Rob grinned. "Yup. It's a hazard of being a SEAL. I just can't get worked up over things after what I've seen and done."

"That's fair," Peyton had to admit. "I'm thinking

Pecky needs to meet a Navy SEAL and have adventures with him."

The boyish grin that came over Rob's face was adorable. "And he'll be named Snacker?"

"Hmmmm," Peyton pretended to think. "Nope. I think he'll be named 'Handsome Butt.'"

"What?" Rob asked incredulously.

Peyton giggled. "That's what I thought the first time I saw you. That you had the best ass I'd ever seen. Maybe Pecky will call his new friend 'Some Butt' instead."

"You wouldn't dare," Rob threatened as he dug his fingers into her sides.

It didn't actually tickle as the wet suit prevented her from really feeling his fingers, but Peyton squirmed in his grip anyway.

He kissed her again, and when he lifted his head, the boat that had been headed their way was almost on top of them. Peyton tensed involuntarily. Rob had said he was sure this was the good guys, but the memory of looking up as the other boat raced above their heads was too clear.

Rob raised his arm and had his hand in a fist as the boat neared.

A shout came from the zodiac and it slowed, coming at them much slower.

"Told you," Rob said with a smile as he looked at her.

"Yeah, you did."

"Hey! Tex called and said you might need a ride. Looks like he was right," An older man with hair much longer than Rob's and a graying beard said with a smile as he maneuvered the boat closer.

"Baker!" Rob exclaimed. "Never thought I'd see *you* out here."

"Well, the other guys are on a mission, and they're gonna be pissed they missed out on fishing you out of the ocean for sure. And for the record, you owe me. I was minding my own business, watching the sweetest woman I've ever met hang out with some high school surfers when I got word that you needed assistance."

"Come on, sweetheart, let's get you out of the water," Rob told Peyton.

She looked up at the boat and shook her head. From a distance, the zodiac didn't look that big, but from right next to it, there was no way she was going to be able to get into the thing. But almost as soon as she had the thought, the man named Baker had grabbed her arms and pulled upward at the same time Rob placed his hand on her ass and pushed.

She was sitting in the bottom of the zodiac before she had time to take a breath. And then Rob was there next to her. He'd pulled himself up and over the side of the boat as if it was child's play. He immediately ripped off his face mask, shrugged off the air bottle on his back and sat next to her on the bottom of the boat. He put his arm around her and pulled her into his side.

Baker passed an emergency blanket folded into a small square to him and within seconds Rob had put it around her shoulders.

"Water?" Baker asked, holding out a bottle.

Peyton grabbed it and was guzzling down the best tasting water she'd ever tasted in her life. It was Rob's low, "Easy, hon," that made her slow down.

She looked at him sheepishly. "Want some?" she asked.

Rob chuckled. "I've got my own. Just don't want you throw that up from drinking too fast," he told her.

Baker had already turned the zodiac around and was headed back toward Oahu at a much slower pace than he'd arrived.

"So...a sweet girl?" Rob asked Baker. "I didn't think you were dating anyone."

"I'm not."

"But you want to," Rob said.

Baker shrugged. "It's complicated."

"As complicated as us having to figure out which

of our exs was mad enough to want us dead?" Rob asked.

Baker snorted. "No."

"When you know, you know," Rob went on, and Peyton felt his gaze on her. "Life's short, man. Don't wait."

The man standing at the back of the boat controlling the engine and steering was hot. He had the whole silver fox thing down pat. But he wasn't the man who made Peyton's heart beat faster. Wasn't the man who she wanted to be with.

"Don't mind me," Baker drawled. "If you two want to get it on, I'll pretend I didn't see anything. I'll even take the long way back to the dock if you want."

"Shut up," Rob told him, but didn't take his gaze from Peyton. "Hang in there, we'll be back before you know it."

She nodded. She should be nervous about what would happen next. If Douchecanoe would try to kill her again when he found out she was alive. Or if Rob's ex would. Of what would happen when they got back to either her room or his. But she wasn't. Rob would figure out who was responsible for what happened and take care of it. He was a man who got things done. And she wanted to be one more of those things that he "did."

.   .   .

* * *

"Thanks, man," Rob said, shaking Baker's hand after they'd arrived at the small marina. Baker had called in a favor and a sailor was waiting in the parking lot to take them wherever they wanted to go. Peyton was standing about twenty feet away, waiting for him, giving him space and privacy to talk to his friend. She didn't have to do that, but he appreciated her consideration anyway.

"No thanks needed," Baker told them. "And you should know, Tex is already on this. He knows all about your girlfriend being the heir to the Crown Condom dynasty, about her ex and yours too. He's taking care of it."

"Was it Douchecanoe or Bertie?" Rob asked.

"Don't know. Does it matter?"

"Not really. Although I'd like to know to be prepared for any surprises in the future."

"There won't be any surprises. You know Tex. He doesn't leave any loose ends."

"Right. Again, thank you."

"Whatever. If I hurry, I can get back to the beach and see Jodelle before she takes off."

"I was serious earlier," Rob told Baker. "You shouldn't wait. Tell her how you feel."

"Now's not the time...but I'm thinking you're right."

"Of course I am," Rob said with a grin.

Baker rolled his eyes. "Why are SEALs so cocky?"

"You should know as you were one too," Rob retorted.

"Go. Get your woman warm. Feed her too while you're at it. And make sure she drinks plenty."

"I know how to take care of Peyton," Rob told him. "Later."

"Later," Baker said, then jumped back into the zodiac and prepared to head away from the dock.

Rob didn't know where he was going, but his attention wasn't on the legendary former SEAL anymore. It was on Peyton. She still had the emergency metallic blanket wrapped around her, was still wearing the shorty wetsuit. Her hair was in a riot around her face from it drying in the wind on the way back to land. Her cheeks were red from the sun and probably the salt and wind as well. He'd never seen anyone as beautiful as she was at that moment.

He strode up the wooden deck toward her and pulled her into his embrace when he reached her.

"Everything all right?" she asked as her hands rested on his chest.

"Yeah. Are we going to your hotel or mine?" he asked, not beating around the bush.

"I don't know. Where are you staying?"

"The Holiday Inn on Waikiki."

She wrinkled her nose and it was all Rob could do not to kiss her. "Mine then. I'm at the Hilton. I have a corner suite with an ocean view."

Rob chuckled. "Yours it is."

"But we can stop by your hotel so you can get your stuff if you want."

"I don't need anything."

Her eyes widened. "Um, Rob, you're wearing a wet suit."

"Yup. And soon I *won't* be wearing it. Maybe I should've said, I don't need anything tonight. Anything but a shower, food, a bed, and you...if that's still okay," he tacked on a little belatedly. They'd been in an intense situation together, and she might be having second thoughts about being with him now that they were on dry land again and safe.

In response, she grabbed his hand and turned toward the man waiting for them in his SUV. She towed him toward the vehicle and opened the door. "In," she ordered.

Rob grinned. "Yes, ma'am," he said obediently.

He had no idea what time it was by the time they'd arrived at her hotel, showered, ate the huge dinner from Duke's Restaurant, including their specialty hula pie for dessert, he'd ordered via delivery, and climbed under the covers.

She was as naked as he was and scooted over until she had her head on his shoulder and her arm over his chest. Rob had never felt as content as he was right that second.

"Rob?"

"Yeah, Pey?"

He felt her smile against him at the shortening of her name, but didn't comment on it. "Are we safe? I mean, we don't know who paid who to do what."

"We're safe," Rob reassured her, kicking his own butt for not having this conversation earlier. "The guy who tracked us? His name is Tex. He lives in Pennsylvania, but he's a computer genius. He's taking care of it for us."

"Okay."

Rob frowned. He lifted his head and tried to meet Peyton's gaze. But she was lying on him almost boneless with her eyes closed. "Okay? That's all you're going to say?"

"Yup. You told me I could trust you, and you were right. About everything. About staying calm, about someone coming for us, about going underwater and sharing air, about that boat that would've done bad things to us, about it all. You made sure I was warm, fed, drank fourteen gallons of water, and gave me time to get under the covers naked before you ditched the bathrobe and came out of the bathroom bare ass naked yourself. If you say your friend Tex has this under control, I believe you."

Rob closed his eyes. Earlier he'd told her that he was lucky, but that word almost seemed too tame for what he was feeling right now. He'd all but given up on love, but it had knocked him on his ass anyway.

"But that doesn't mean I'm not writing Bertie and Douchecanoe into one of my cartoons and making Pecky embarrass the crap out of them," she warned.

Rob chuckled. "Can't wait to see what you have planned for them." After a moment he added firmly, "This is going to work. You and me. It's gonna work." It was too soon to tell Peyton that he loved her, but he did. He knew it as well as he knew the SEAL manual...and he had that damn thing memorized.

"It is," she agreed. Then she sighed. "Rob?"

"Yeah, hon?"

"I want you. I want you so deep inside me I don't know where I start and you begin. I want you to make me come and I want to do the same to you. I want to taste you, memorize that handsome butt I'm so enamored with. I want to be on top and on bottom, and have you take me from behind and any other way we can think of. I want it all..."

Rob was hard from her first three words, but had only gotten harder as she continued to speak.

"...but I'm too tired to appreciate all that is you tonight. Is that...okay?"

And just like that, his erection softened. Not all the way, but enough that he didn't feel as if he was being turned inside out. "Yes," he said. He was tired himself. Exhausted. And while he could've made their lovemaking amazing for her, he wanted their first time to be when they weren't both dead on their feet...or backs.

"The shower..." she said. "...it was amazing. You really are a handsome butt. And chest, and arms, and cock, and legs, and I want to examine those tattoos closer...when I can keep my eyes open."

Rob chuckled. His woman was funny when she was half asleep.

"Sleep, Pey. You can examine me tomorrow."

"Good. Can we find a taco truck tomorrow too? I never did get my tacos the captain promised," she grumbled.

"We can do anything you want tomorrow."

"Good. I have some Pecky cartoons to draw too."

Rob winced. He wasn't sure if she was kidding or not when she'd talked about having Pecky the taco meet a Navy SEAL he nicknamed 'Some Butt' or not. "Okay."

To his surprise, Peyton's eyes opened and she came up on an elbow. He could feel her nipple against his naked chest, her curves pressed up against his side, and he never felt so content. She leaned into him and kissed him gently. It wasn't a passionate kiss, not like the ones they'd shared earlier when they were in the shower. It was a mere brushing of her lips against his. A promise.

"It wasn't you who was lucky today. It was me. And I know it. I'll never take you for granted. I'll support you no matter where your Navy career takes you. I'll never cheat on you or ask you for anything you can't give."

"I'll give you anything and *everything*," Rob returned. "And you thinking you're the lucky one is adorable. You're wrong, but you can think that if you want."

She huffed out a breath and collapsed back down on him. "Whatever."

Rob shifted until he could tangle his fingers in his hair as he held her against him. He had a momentary vision of them lying just like this years from now. After their kids were grown and out of the house, after he was retired, and after they were well past what society deemed was the "prime" of their lives. He had no doubt they'd be just as content and in love as they were right this second. And there was no doubt he loved this woman and he knew she loved him back. It wasn't the time or place to reveal their feelings, but he had no doubt they had a long and fulfilling life in their future.

"*Ummmm*," she murmured as she snuggled into his side.

'*Ummmm* indeed,' he thought right before he fell into a deep sleep with his woman safe in his arms.

TRUSTING WILLIS

by Susan Stoker

ABOUT THE BOOK:

A Brand new novella featuring Gregory Willis...the FBI contact first seen in the Silverstone series.

Since the brutal murder of his wife and daughter, FBI agent Gregory Willis has used every resource in his arsenal to hunt down the worst of humanity. He couldn't save his loved ones, but he tirelessly prevents as many needless deaths as possible through teams of unsanctioned, off-the-books mercenaries. When he's finally ordered to take some much-needed time off, he begins to take note of someone much closer to home—his neighbor, Maylah Brant. Especially when he spots her getting out of a taxi, her own vehicle nowhere in sight and the woman clearly injured.

He spends his vacation getting to know his pretty neighbor and tracking down the carjacker who had more than simple theft on his mind—and wants to finish the job. Gregory already lost one woman he loves. He won't risk losing another.

CHAPTER ONE

GREGORY WILLIS WAS TIRED.

He'd spent the day making sure everything at work was wrapped up before the mandatory three weeks off his boss was making him take.

Working in the FBI's intelligence sector had been at turns a dream come true, and a nightmare. The worst of the latter being when he'd lost his wife and teenage daughter. He'd been too wrapped up in work to accompany them when they wanted to go shopping during a visit to France. They'd ended up kidnapped and tortured—for two long weeks—before their kidnapper finally got tired of his sick game and killed them both.

That was several years ago. Since, Willis had buried himself in his job, working even harder to find and take out the worst humanity had to offer. He'd done anything necessary to make that happen... including hiring teams of assassins. He spent countless hours searching for information to pass on to those who could end the lives of the terrorists, murderers, sex traffickers, and other men and women who did their best to destroy the innocent.

The Department of Justice had a "black" budget that Willis had appropriated to finance the groups of men he employed. At the moment, however, there were no active missions, which was a very rare occurrence. And the reason why Willis had been told in no uncertain terms to take time off. Maybe take a trip somewhere. Relax.

Willis didn't know the meaning of the word. There were *always* terrorists to track down. Innocent women and children to rescue. Those similar to his wife and daughter. Willis hadn't been able to save his loved ones, but over the years, he was proud that the people he'd hired had saved almost four hundred innocent souls who'd been held hostage or kidnapped.

For the most part, no one would ever know he was the man behind their rescues. He was a silent partner, the one providing the intel and money the mercenaries needed to go in and do the dirty work.

This was the first time in years that Willis had taken any time off. He had no family waiting at home—or anywhere else. Nothing to look forward to when he left his office in the FBI headquarters building in Washington, DC. Three weeks of unending boredom loomed ahead of him, and Willis dreaded it. When he wasn't busy, that was when the memories of his wife and daughter pressed in on him the most. And he couldn't help but think of all the others who were out there in the world, desperately in need of rescuing...people he might miss because he was sitting at home, twiddling his damn thumbs.

Sighing, Willis headed for the stairs that led up to his brownstone. He lived in an older section of the city in a remodeled townhome that was just one in a full city block. He really didn't talk to any of his neighbors; he saw them now and then as he came and went. They were friendly enough, took good care of their property...which was all he cared to know.

It was now dark outside, nearing nine o'clock, and Willis wasn't surprised he was the only one out and about. The entire area was well-lit and quiet, and he'd never felt unsafe in the neighborhood.

He'd just put the key in the lock at his front door when he heard a vehicle behind him.

Glancing behind him to see who it was, Willis was somewhat surprised to see a taxi pull up in front of the brownstone two doors down from his own.

Tilting his head, he observed quietly as his neighbor struggled to climb out of the backseat.

Maylah Brant was a widow, like him. He might not know his neighbors personally—but he still made the effort to look into each and every one of the people living in the brownstones around him. It made him an asshole. He knew that. But the last thing he wanted was to live in an area where his neighbors might want to do him harm. To his relief, all of them seemed to be unassuming, law-abiding men and women simply going about their lives.

Maylah lived alone. Her husband had passed away unexpectedly about ten years ago of a heart attack. They hadn't had any children, and she lived a quiet and unassuming life with the money her husband had left to her in the form of life insurance and investments. He had no idea what she did to pass the time, as she didn't seem to have a full-time job. At least, not one he knew about.

At the moment, Willis wasn't thinking about any of that. All he could see was a woman struggling to stand, and the man behind the wheel not doing a damn thing to help. In fact, the taxi driver was drumming his fingers on the steering wheel impatiently.

Willis moved before he thought about what he was doing. He was down the eight or so steps that led up to his door and at her side within seconds.

"Let me help," he said gently, as he took Maylah's elbow in his hand. He felt her immediately lean on him as she looked up. Her blue eyes were hazy with pain, and she blinked in gratitude.

"Thanks," she said softly.

Willis felt as if he'd been hit by a two-by-four.

Of course he'd noticed his neighbor. He'd nodded at her as she walked a dog—a different dog almost every time he saw her. Brief, nonverbal exchanges. But standing here in the dark evening, the woman leaning on him for balance...and touching her for the first time...Willis suddenly felt off balance.

"Close the door!" the taxi driver called out from the front seat.

Willis forced himself not to lash out at the man. He focused on Maylah. "Do you have everything?"

She let out a small huff, which was a mix of a snort and a laugh. "Yeah," she told him.

Willis took a step away from the taxi, keeping a firm grip on the unsteady woman in front of him, and shut the car door. Within seconds, the taxi pulled away from the curb, leaving Willis alone with Maylah.

"Where's your car?" he blurted.

Maylah sighed. "I don't know."

Willis blinked. "What do you mean, you don't know?"

"Just that," she said. "I'd just finished getting gas

and was about to get back into it, when someone rushed up and held a gun to my face and told me to get in."

Every muscle in Willis' body tightened. "*What?*"

"Yeah, I was surprised too. I mean, I know it happens, but I still never expected to be carjacked. I did what he asked and got back into the car, then he forced me to scoot over and he got behind the wheel. It all happened so fast. Like...within seconds. He drove off with me in the passenger seat. I knew nothing good could possibly happen once he got me to wherever he was going, so as we were going around a corner, I opened the door and bailed."

"What?!" Willis asked again, knowing he sounded ridiculous asking the same question over and over, but he couldn't wrap his brain around what Maylah was telling him.

She smiled a little, and just that small quirk of her lips made Willis feel weird deep down inside.

"I jumped out of a moving car. It wasn't the smartest thing I've ever done. Luckily, there was a family on the corner where I ended up, waiting to cross, and they called the police for me. Nothing was broken, thankfully. I just have a bad case of road rash and a minor concussion where I hit my head on the street when I landed. Seems to be causing some dizziness and balance issues. Anyway, I was in the emergency room forever and was discharged just a bit ago."

Willis shook his head in disbelief. "You should still be there. Head wounds aren't anything to mess around with."

"I couldn't. I just got a new foster. She's probably already peed on the floor and is most likely freaked out at being left alone for so long. I actually went out to get food and a new bed for her. I was only supposed to be gone for thirty minutes, tops. It's been hours."

There was so much he wanted to say, but the need to get this woman inside and safe was stronger than his need to get the answers to his many questions. Turning, he headed for the stairs that led up to her brownstone. It was slow going, as her steps were hesitant and unsteady. Willis wanted to wrap his arm around her waist, to brace her better, but he didn't want to upset her by touching her too intimately. So his hand tightened on her arm as he patiently walked her up the stairs.

"Well...thanks for helping me," she sighed.

Willis frowned. "Where's your purse?" he asked. "Your keys?"

"In my car...wherever that is by now."

His first thought was that the carjacker now had access to her address and her house because he had her keys and wallet with her ID, but he didn't want to scare the living daylights out of Maylah by mentioning that. So instead he asked, "How are you going to get in?"

Maylah gave him another small smile. "I'm forever locking myself out. I always forget to grab my keys when I take one of my fosters for a walk, so I've made sure to keep one out here."

She stepped away from Willis, and he kept his eye on her to make sure she didn't fall over as she reached into one of the many potted plants on her front stoop. She grinned at him wryly as she straightened and held up a key.

Willis wanted to lecture her on how unsafe it was to keep a spare key in a hiding place that was easy for someone with nefarious intentions to find. But instead, he asked, "May I?" while nodding to the key.

She nodded and held it out to him.

Willis took it and put it in the lock, then swung her door open and gestured for her to head inside.

"Thanks. Um...do you want to come in?"

He should say no. Should let her get some rest. But for some reason, he didn't want to end his interaction with her. Didn't want to go home to his silent and empty townhouse. And it was obvious she was still unsteady on her feet. If she fell and hurt herself further, he'd never forgive himself. Not to mention the asshole who stole her car had her keys. He nodded.

It took everything within him not to reach for her when she stumbled a little as she went through the door. Once they were inside, Willis made sure the door was shut tightly and locked behind them, then he followed Maylah through the small foyer as she headed into her home.

"You're Greg, right?" she asked.

Willis blinked. No one called him Greg. Every once in a while someone used his full first name, Gregory, but mostly everyone used his last name. Regardless, he nodded.

"I see you all the time, but we haven't really had a chance to talk. I'm Maylah Brant. It's nice to officially meet you."

Willis nodded. He was acting odd and he knew it, but for some reason, he was having a hard time speaking like a normal human being. Couldn't find the right words. He was saved from the awkwardness by a whine coming from a corner of the room.

Tensing, Willis took a step forward, putting himself between Maylah and whatever or whoever had made the sound.

But Maylah put a hand on his back and scooted around him. "I'm so sorry, baby. I didn't mean to be gone so long. Are you okay? Did you explore while I was gone? Were you scared?"

Willis could still feel the heat from where she'd touched him. It felt like a brand on his back. It was confusing as hell, and not understanding what was happening to him made him want to turn around and leave immediately. Instead, he straightened his spine. He wasn't a coward, and he didn't want to leave this woman before making sure she was all right.

He couldn't get the disturbing image of Maylah throwing herself out of a moving car out of his mind.

His neighbor stepped forward and stumbled yet again. Thankfully, there was a love seat next to her when she lost her balance, and she fell onto the cushions. The quick movements made the creature in the corner cower backward, another pathetic little whimper escaping its throat.

When Maylah tried to get up, Willis finally snapped himself out of his stupor.

"Stay," he ordered, holding up a hand, palm toward her.

To his relief, she rolled her eyes, but didn't try to get up. Willis moved toward the corner, stopping when he was several feet away. He crouched down and finally got a good look at the animal. It was a dog. At least, he thought it was. The animal had matted black hair, and two small brown eyes blinked up at him as she cowered in fear.

Seeing the poor creature so terrified made Willis react almost viscerally. He'd seen more than his share of body cam videos from rescues he'd arranged. Many of the women and children, and the occasional man, had reacted the same way toward their rescuers. They'd been abused and hurt, and they always expected more of the same.

Moving slowly, Willis sat on the floor and crossed his legs. With no thought other than trying to make the dog feel safe, he unbuttoned the suit jacket he was wearing and held out a hand. Then he began to murmur nonsense to the dog. Telling her she was safe, that Maylah wouldn't hurt her. That she had found the absolute best place to heal and learn to trust again.

He had no idea how long he sat there talking quietly to the mutt, but when she finally stretched her neck out to sniff at his fingers, Willis had never felt so relieved.

"You're good at that," Maylah said quietly from behind him. "It usually takes me days to get a new foster to trust me even a little."

"What's her story?" Willis asked, not looking away from the black ball of fluff.

"Found on the streets. The vet said she had a few

broken ribs, probably from being kicked. She's obviously been starving. It looks as if she had at least one litter of puppies, but none were found around where *she* was in an alley."

"Her name?"

"She doesn't have one yet," Maylah said. "I usually wait a few days before naming them so I can get to know them. Their personality and quirks."

"Princess," Willis blurted.

"What?"

"Her name. She needs to know she's beautiful, just like a princess."

Silence filled the room, and Willis closed his eyes for a moment before opening them and turning his head to look behind him. "Sorry. It's just a suggestion. You've done this way longer than I have, you can name her whatever you—"

"Princess is perfect," she interrupted.

Willis turned back around when he felt something cold on his fingers. Princess had crept out of the corner she'd been cowering in and was nuzzling his fingers. Then she shocked the crap out of him when she moved closer, crawling up and over his knee and settling into his lap.

In shock, Willis turned once again to Maylah.

She was grinning from ear to ear. "Looks like you have a new friend."

Willis wanted to protest. But he couldn't deny it felt really good that the dog trusted him. As much as he wanted to sit on the floor with Princess, the pained look in Maylah's eyes made him ask, "Does she have a leash?" His neighbor clearly couldn't walk this dog at the moment.

Maylah nodded. "The one that came from the rescue group is hanging in the foyer by the front door on a hook."

Willis moved slowly, scooping Princess up in his arms and standing. To his surprise, the dog didn't whimper or shake, simply let him hold her. "I'll be back."

"What?" Maylah asked.

"I'll take her out, see if she'll do her business. Then I'll be back to clean up the mess on the floor," he said, nodding to a small puddle near where the dog had been cowering. "I can make her some chicken and rice to tide her over until we can get some dog food for her."

"Oh, but...um...I don't..."

Willis grinned at her obvious confusion. "I'll be back," he said firmly, then turned for the door.

CHAPTER TWO

MAYLAH STARED at her neighbor's ass as he walked toward her front door with her newest foster in his arms. This wasn't how she thought this day would end. Hell, nothing had gone the way she'd expected it to today. Being carjacked wasn't on her agenda, wasn't something she thought she'd ever have to experience. She didn't drive a fancy car, had been at that gas station in the middle of the day, and she wasn't exactly the kind of woman she figured anyone would want to kidnap.

She was forty-eight and wasn't what she would call beautiful...or even pretty. Her nose was too big, she was on the short side, her hair was never styled and she rarely wore makeup. She was too heavy, too average, too...boring.

Not only that, but she'd aged a lot in the ten years

since her husband had died. It had been extremely difficult to get back on her feet after losing Ted. He was a good man, and they'd had a nice if not very exciting life. She'd been content. Finding her husband dead on the floor of their kitchen from a sudden heart attack had been a shock she wasn't able to shake for years.

It wasn't until recently, in the last two years or so, that Maylah had felt more like herself again. She'd found a purpose in fostering dogs and cats for a local rescue group. It felt really good to take in a scared and confused animal and help it gain confidence. And finding them loving homes was icing on the cake. But in truth, the animals healed her as much as she healed them.

When she'd left home that afternoon to get food and a bed for her newest foster, she hadn't expected to find herself in the middle of a carjacking. And she'd insisted on checking herself out of the hospital because of the dog waiting for her at home.

But honestly, she felt awful. Her head hurt and she had a nasty case of road rash along the right side of her body, where she'd landed. She was unsteady on her feet, and on top of all that, the police had scared the crap out of her by reminding her that whoever had taken her car, also had her purse—with her keys and identification. He knew where she lived.

The detectives had reassured her that it was unlikely he'd come to her house; that in their experience, thieves took money and credit cards then dumped the purse in a dumpster somewhere. But Maylah couldn't stop thinking about the fact that the man who'd stolen her car had looked at her with lust in his eyes. He wanted more than her car, she was sure of it—which was why she'd bailed out without a second thought.

To try to block out the memory of the evil look in the carjacker's eyes, Maylah instead turned her thoughts to her neighbor. She'd noticed him before, of course. He looked nothing like her husband. Greg was a few inches shorter, and not nearly as muscular. While Ted had stood out wherever they went because of his good looks, his size, and his outgoing personality, Greg was the opposite. He never smiled much, always wore a business suit, and didn't seem social at all.

Regardless, there was something about the man that made Maylah immediately trust him. She thought about the dog. Princess instinctually saw the same thing. The way she'd immediately crawled into his lap was a clear indication.

Greg Willis might look like he was a math teacher, or someone who liked to play chess or Dungeons and Dragons in his spare time, but there was an undercurrent of something undefinable that appealed to Maylah. Something steadfast and trustworthy. And dangerous...but in a different way than her carjacker. It was as if the man wore a business suit to hide the fact that he was a black belt in karate or an expert at knife throwing.

It made no sense, but no matter how much Maylah tried to shake off the thought, she couldn't help but think there was a lot more to the man than what he wanted the world to see.

Closing her eyes, she sighed. She needed to get up, clean the floor, start the rice for Princess' dinner. But she felt so weak. Shaky. Today had scared her. A lot. She hadn't felt fear like that since she'd found Ted unresponsive on their kitchen floor.

Unknown minutes later, the sound of her door opening made her jerk awake and sit up to look over the back of the love seat. There was a small entryway just inside the door, out of sight from the large open space she now sat in. She sighed in relief when Greg appeared from around the corner. Princess was nestled in the crook of one of his arms, as if she was perfectly content to stay there forever.

"What's wrong? Is it your head? Do I need to call an ambulance?" Greg asked as he walked toward her.

"What? No, I'm fine."

"You look freaked out," he said. "And like you're in pain."

"I must've fallen asleep," Maylah told him. "I heard the door and for a second thought... Anyway, I'm okay."

Greg's lips pressed together as he stared at her.

For some reason, Maylah wanted to reassure him. "I'm really okay. Honest. Did she do her business?"

After a brief pause, Greg nodded. "Yeah. Took a while, since every sound seemed to scare her to death, but eventually she did."

"Good. I appreciate you helping out, but I'm sure you have stuff to do. I can—"

"I don't," Greg said, interrupting her.

"Pardon?"

"I don't have anything to do. My boss kicked me out of the office and told me not to come back for three weeks. I'm on vacation, and I have no idea what to do with myself."

Maylah tried to hold back the smile at seeing how disgruntled he seemed at being forced to taking a vacation. "I'm not surprised. I had you pegged as a workaholic," she told him.

"Yeah," he agreed without an ounce of dismay. "So...I have nothing to do at home but stare at my walls. If you'd be comfortable with me staying, I wouldn't mind making Princess something to eat."

How could she say no to that? "Okay."

"Okay," he agreed with a small smile. "Are you hungry?"

"Me? Oh, I'm good," Maylah said.

"When's the last time you ate? Did the doctor give you painkillers at the hospital? You shouldn't take that on an empty stomach. I'm not a gourmet cook, but I can manage to bake chicken. If you don't have any, I've got some at my place. I can run over and get it."

He seemed so eager. So earnest. "Um...I don't know if I have any chicken, but I'm sure I have something you can feed Princess."

Greg stared at her for a long moment. Maylah once again had the thought this man wasn't anything like Ted. She'd always been able to deflect his concerns over her by changing the subject. But Greg simply raised a brow as he stared, waiting.

"I had lunch," she said a little defensively.

Greg still didn't speak.

Feeling uneasy with the silence, Maylah kept talking. "A grilled cheese sandwich. With tomato. And a pickle spear."

His lips twitched.

Maylah sighed. "Fine. I could eat. And yeah, I feel a little nauseous from the meds."

Greg nodded. "I'll be right back. Don't get up. I

mean it. Here...take Princess." He took a step toward her and placed the dog in her lap.

Surprised, Maylah brought her hands up and held onto the pitiful little creature. She was a mutt through and through. The rescue group thought maybe she was a mix of Yorkshire terrier, Maltese, and beagle. Princess trembled, but didn't try to get out of her grip.

Without another word, Greg once more headed for her front door. The second it closed behind him, Maylah let out a small breath. "What is it about him?" she asked the dog in her lap. But Princess stayed silent.

Eventually, Princess' shaking stopped and she fell asleep in Maylah's lap. Once again, Maylah was dozing when the door to her townhome opened. She was pleased that she didn't jump as much this time, simply looked over to the foyer, expecting to see Greg.

She wasn't wrong, but she frowned when he appeared. He was carrying a large plastic tub...filled with way more than just a few chicken breasts from his fridge.

He walked into the living area and put the tub down on her coffee table. He pulled out two pillows and a large comforter. He placed them on the floor, arranging them until he was satisfied. He headed in her direction, and sat on the cushion next to her.

"She do okay?" he asked, tilting his head in Princess' direction.

"Yeah. She fell asleep."

"Good. May I?" he asked once again, nodding at the dog.

Maylah lifted her hands off Princess and nodded.

Very carefully, Greg picked up the sleeping dog. He murmured to her as he moved toward the comforter and pillows. Then he placed her on them gently and stayed crouched down as he continued to speak in a voice too low for Maylah to hear. She smiled as Princess woke up enough to start plumping the covers to her satisfaction. The dog let out a long sigh of approval as she curled into a tiny ball in the middle of the soft nest.

Only then did Greg stand. He went back to the tub, picked it up, and headed for her kitchen.

Bemused, Maylah could only watch as he took item after item out of the tub and placed it on the counter. It took him a moment to orient himself in her kitchen, to find what he needed, but it was more than obvious he didn't need her help because soon he had a pot of water with rice boiling away on the stove.

It wasn't until he came into the room and

crouched down to wipe up the floor that Maylah stirred. "I can do that," she informed him.

"I know, but you aren't. Stay there and rest," Greg said.

If she'd heard any hint of irritation that he was wiping pee from the floor, Maylah would've insisted she help, but her neighbor seemed perfectly willing to do it himself. It was surprising how comfortable she was with Greg in her home. She didn't have a lot of friends, had kept to herself since Ted died. So it should've felt weird to have someone else in her space, cooking in her kitchen, cleaning up after the dog. But instead it felt... comfortable. Safe.

For a third time, Maylah must've fallen asleep because the next thing she knew, Greg was saying her name. Opening her eyes, she saw he was sitting next to her on the couch and held a bowl with rice and diced chicken. And the food smelled absolutely delicious.

She glanced at her watch and saw that it was almost eleven. She felt a twinge of guilt that she'd kept him up so late, but then remembered what he said about being on vacation. More than that, she remembered the look of discomfort on his face when he'd admitted that he had absolutely nothing to do for the next three weeks.

"This smells and looks delicious," she said as she scooted up on the cushions.

Greg shrugged. "It's not anything special, but it'll fill you up."

He handed her the bowl, and when their fingers brushed against each other, Maylah shivered in reaction. He was so warm, and little bolts of electricity went from her fingers to what felt like straight to her heart. Her gaze dropped from his as she tried to understand what was happening.

She spotted Princess on the floor, still in her little nest, chowing down without swallowing what looked like the same thing she was about to eat.

"Wait, are you feeding me dog food?" she teased.

Greg smiled. "Nope. Princess is getting people food," he said with a shrug. Then he stood and headed back to the kitchen.

Maylah watched as he fixed himself a bowl, somehow not surprised he'd fed both her and Princess before himself. He took his bowl to her small kitchen table and pulled out a chair.

"Oh, please, don't eat over there by yourself," Maylah blurted.

Greg stared at her for a beat, then nodded and pushed the chair back under the table. He walked back to the love seat and, to her surprise, sat on the floor at her feet, leaning back against the cushions.

That wasn't exactly what she'd meant, but at least he wasn't on the other side of the room anymore.

They ate in silence, but it was a comfortable one. Maylah didn't feel a need to fill the air with meaningless chatter. Even though this man, her neighbor, someone she'd smiled at many times and seen from inside her house as he left early in the morning and came back late at night, felt more like an old friend than a complete stranger.

She hadn't been wrong, the chicken and rice was very good. Whatever he'd spiced it with was delicious, giving the bland rice a somewhat smokey taste. The chicken was also perfectly baked and seasoned.

He finished about the same time as she did, but didn't make a move to get up. He put his bowl on the floor next to him and sighed.

Maylah was about to thank him again and tell him he could go home, when Princess moved from her spot in the corner. She slunk toward Greg, sniffing his empty bowl, then crawled back into his lap.

She'd already trusted this man, but seeing how strongly the dog was drawn to him went a long way toward reassuring Maylah that she wasn't being stupid. She trusted the reactions of her fosters more than she did most people.

She'd been terrified today. Had seen her life flash before her eyes. Now, it was hard to believe that it was just a few hours ago that she'd been in a life-or-death situation.

After a short while, Greg said, "I should go."

Maylah couldn't bring herself to agree. It was surprising that she didn't really want him to leave. But instead, she simply whispered, "Okay."

Greg stood and brought Princess back to her corner, then returned to the couch and collected both their bowls. He went back to the kitchen and started to clean up.

"I can do that," she protested.

But of course her houseguest simply shrugged and ignored her, continuing to load her dishwasher with all the dirty dishes he'd used to make their dinner.

He was almost done when there was a sound in the direction of her front door.

Looking at the foyer, Maylah was confused for a moment. When she looked at Greg, he'd gone stock still. He lifted a finger to his lips, telling her to stay quiet, and slowly made his way around the counter toward the foyer.

Maylah wanted to tell him to stop. Not to go *toward* the door, but away from it. But she couldn't speak. Just like earlier that day, she was frozen in fear.

She heard the door swing open and heard a heavy footstep enter her house. A man appeared from the entryway. He was dressed all in black. The person—

she assumed it was a man by his height and build—had a mask pulled over his face...and she saw a knife in his hand. It glinted in the light coming from her apartment.

They locked eyes and Maylah's blood ran cold. His eyes were dark, just like the clothes he was wearing, and she swore she recognized the evil look before he turned his head in Greg's direction. He jolted in surprise as Greg leaped toward him.

Greg managed to grab hold of the man's sweatshirt, but the intruder jerked away from him. Without hesitation, he turned and disappeared back into the foyer. There was a slight scuffling noise out of Maylah's sight and she abruptly stood, frantically looking around for her phone, before remembering that it was in her purse which had been in her car.

Before she had time to do more than start to panic, she heard her front door slam closed. Every muscle in her body sagged in relief when Greg reappeared from the small entryway and stalked toward her.

She blinked in surprise when he said, "Good girl." It wasn't until Greg came around the edge of the love seat that she even realized Princess had left her corner and gone to Greg's side. She was shaking, but also growling low in her throat.

Maylah wanted to cry. Cry because a man had

entered her house with a knife. In relief because Greg wasn't hurt and had chased the man away. Because the foster dog she'd had for less than a day seemed to want to protect her. Because Greg had taken the time to acknowledge and praise the obviously emotionally abused animal. Basically, she felt as if she was falling apart.

Greg didn't say anything, simply leaned down and put one arm under her knees, the other around her back, and picked her up.

"Greg?" she asked as she wound her arms around his neck.

"You're not staying here," he said gruffly. "That asshole used a key—*your* key—to get inside."

"I don't know where to go," she said in shock.

Greg stared at her a moment before walking toward the back door without a word. He opened it and looked out cautiously for a moment before step-ping outside. Looking down, Maylah saw Princess at Greg's heels. She wasn't letting him out of her sight, not that she could blame the little dog. At the moment, she didn't want to let her neighbor go either.

"Where are we going?" she asked, trying to take her mind off what had just happened and the pain of her injuries from being carried.

"My place."

She blinked in surprise. She'd expected him to say he was taking her to a hotel or something. "Is that a good idea? I mean, you only live a few doors down. And I don't want to put you in danger."

He snorted but didn't reply as he strode through the grassy yards behind the brownstones. No one had fences, the residents had all gotten together and decided to share the area behind the buildings. There were picnic tables and a couple of grills, but Greg didn't slow down as he headed for his own back door.

Within minutes, they were inside his house and he was walking up the stairs, Princess doing her best to keep up.

"Greg?" she said.

He didn't answer.

"Greg?" she tried again. "I can walk."

"I know," he said. Still, he didn't put her down.

Maylah had to admit, she wasn't sure she *could* walk at the moment. Too many 'what-ifs' were swirling around in her head. What if she'd been home alone? What if she'd been upstairs in bed and hadn't heard the door open? What if the intruder hadn't been scared away by Greg? She knew whoever had carjacked her, had returned. She'd gotten away from him, and he wasn't happy. She didn't know *why* he was so determined to carry out his plans, but he clearly was.

She recalled the knife she'd seen in his hand, and shivered. Greg's arms tightened around her as he entered what could only be his bedroom. He placed her gently on the mattress then fussed with the covers, just as he'd done with Princess' bed earlier.

Finally, he bent down and picked up the dog who hadn't left his side and placed her on top of the covers next to Maylah.

"Stay here," he ordered.

She began to sit up, but Greg's hand landed on her shoulder, holding her still.

"I need to—"

"You need to stay here," he ordered gruffly. "I'll take care of this."

Maylah was a little irritated at being ordered around, but she had to admit that she didn't have the first clue what she should do right about now. "I should call the police."

"I'm going to do that. I'll go back over to your place and meet them there."

"They're going to want to talk to me," she insisted.

"They will. But they'll have to wait until tomorrow," Greg told her.

His hand hadn't left her shoulder, and the weight and heat of his fingers felt like a brand. In a good way.

"It was him," she whispered.

"Probably." Greg nodded, not asking who she was talking about. "But you're safe here. And I'm going to fix this."

He'd said that before, but Maylah wasn't sure how. "How?" she blurted.

"I have connections, Maylah. A reputation in both criminal and law enforcement circles. People know better than to cross me. And whoever this is, he's either new to the area and doesn't know who he's messing with, or he's got a death wish."

"But we don't even know each other. I mean, we do, but we aren't...you're my *neighbor*...we don't..." She stumbled over the words, feeling awkward all of a sudden.

"I *am* your neighbor, and no, we don't know each other, but the lowlifes in this town know this is my neighborhood. They also know I take the safety of my surroundings seriously. And, Maylah...we may not have been anything but neighbors before tonight. But now? We're more."

She should've balked at that...but instead, her belly did flip-flops. "We are?" she whispered.

"I hope so. I haven't felt this way toward a woman since my wife died. And I never thought I'd ever feel about *any* woman the way I did about her. Until now."

Greg was so intense. The way he was looking at her should've made Maylah jump off the bed and get the hell out of his house. But she recalled how gentle he was with Princess. How he'd brought over some of his own pillows and blankets to make a bed for the frightened animal. How he'd cooked for not only her, but for the dog as well. How Princess had trusted him implicitly, and even now stared up at him with a look of complete devotion.

And...she felt the same way. When Ted died, a part of her heart died with him. The only thing she'd found pleasure in since his death was fostering animals. Until tonight.

Her heart was beating fast. She felt giddy, and it wasn't because of her concussion.

"Okay," she whispered.

Greg's lips twitched. "Okay?" he asked.

She nodded. "Yeah."

"You'll stay? Here? Let me deal with the cops and your situation?"

"Yes."

Greg's eyes closed for a beat, and when they opened, she saw something in his gaze that made her want to throw her arms around his neck and pull him onto the bed with her.

At one point, she'd actually considered this man cold. He rarely smiled, talked even less, and he seemed to be made out of stone. But the emotion she saw in his eyes right now made it clear he'd been hiding behind an impenetrable shield.

Now, he was anything but cold. Respect, desire, fear, and determination shone in his dark eyes, making him seem so much...*bigger*...than he was a moment ago.

He leaned down, kissed the top of her head, then ran a hand over Princess' fur. "Keep her safe for me," he told the little dog, then spun and headed for the doorway. He turned once he got there. "The bathroom's there," he said with a tilt of his head toward a door to the left of the bed. "I've got T-shirts in the middle drawer, and there's a clean cup in the bathroom along with some over-the-counter painkillers if your head continues to hurt. Get comfortable. I'll be back to check on you after I meet with the cops, get the locks on your place changed, get some food for Princess, and make some calls."

Maylah blinked in surprise. "Change my locks? Get some food...?"

"Yeah."

"But everything's closed right now."

Greg smiled. "Maybe, but as I said...I've got connections. Sleep, Maylah. You're safe here. I give you my word."

Before she could respond, he was gone.

Maylah looked down at the dog at her side and said, "What's happening?"

But Princess wasn't talking.

Sighing, Maylah closed her eyes. She'd get up and change in a moment. For now, she just needed a moment to think. So much had happened in a short period of time, and her head was spinning.

Before she knew it, she'd fallen into a deep sleep, secure in the knowledge that she was safe.

CHAPTER THREE

WILLIS SAT in his living room and sipped the glass of bourbon he'd poured for himself. It was almost four in the morning, but he wasn't tired. Not in the least. He'd called in a favor and gotten Maylah's locks changed, and had a long conversation with the detective who'd come out to her house after being notified about the break-in.

He had many questions—and still many more phone calls to make—but for now, he was content to sit in his dark house and think about the change his life had taken in such a few short hours.

When Elle and Molly died, he didn't think he'd ever love anyone the way he'd loved his wife and daughter again. He couldn't even imagine it. But slowly over the years, the pain faded. It didn't go away, it never would, but he felt as if he had more good days than bad. The guilt would always be there though. He should've taken his girls shopping like they'd begged him to. But work had been more important—and he'd paid the price for that a hundred times over.

Now, for some reason, something about Maylah felt...right. He couldn't ignore her situation. Maybe it was atonement for his family. Maybe it was the twisting of his gut when he realized she'd checked herself out of the hospital for a dog. Whatever it was, instead of being uncomfortable with having someone else in his home, his bed, Willis felt protective and...content.

The memory of the cocky asshole brazenly walking into Maylah's house as if he had every right to be there burned in Willis' gut. Looking at his watch, he decided that he'd waited long enough to take care of this situation. He'd learned the full details of what had happened to Maylah from the detective earlier.

She'd been at the gas station, like she'd said, and a white man, pock marked, clean shaven, a wide nose, dark brown eyes, very short hair, and about six-one or two—the same height as the man who'd shown up at her door earlier—had pushed her into the car and driven off with her. She'd managed to escape because the carjacker had been too confident. He assumed he'd scared her enough to comply with his every demand and hadn't bothered to lock the doors.

The detective was still working to figure out who the carjacker was, looking at surveillance cameras and canvasing the neighborhood where the incident had happened, but Willis had his own connections. He had a feeling he'd be able to get to the bottom of what happened sooner than the detective.

Putting down his glass, Willis pulled out his phone. He didn't care what time it was, he needed intel. He dialed a phone number and waited for the person on the other end to answer.

"What the fuck? Do you know what time it is?" a groggy voice bitched.

"I know exactly what time it is, Boo. What I want to know *now* is who the hell thought it would be a good idea to break into the brownstone two doors down from mine," he growled.

The confidential informant on the other end of the phone cleared his threat. "Willis?" he asked.

"Of course. I need info. And I need it now," Willis threatened.

"I don't know nothin'," Boo whined.

"Well, you better start finding out what I want to know." Willis had no problem using CIs for the information he needed. He used them to make sure the criminal elements on the streets knew not to mess with him. And when he needed intel for a case, the CIs were more than willing to share. "A woman who is now under my protection was carjacked yesterday afternoon. She had to jump out of a damn moving car to get away. Then the asshole decided to use her keys to waltz into her house—which, as I already told you, is in my neighborhood. You *know* this isn't acceptable."

"I don't know anythin' about anythin'—but I'll find out," Boo promised.

"You do that. I expect a call before lunch."

"You'll have it."

Willis clicked the connection off without saying goodbye, then immediately dialed another CI. He had a very similar conversation with him—and with the three people after that.

Satisfied that he'd done what he could to spread the word and to make sure everyone knew Maylah was off limits, Willis leaned back in his chair.

He lived in a gray world. He looked the other way when the people he associated with sold drugs or engaged in other illegal misdemeanors. Willis wasn't concerned with small shit. He cared about human trafficking, people being held against their will, and terrorist plots. His reputation was rock solid in DC. The people he dealt with knew better than to cross him. And right now, he was using their fear to his advantage.

"Greg?"

Jerking in surprise, Willis glanced toward the stairs and saw Maylah standing at the bottom. She had Princess in her arms and was wearing one of his T-shirts. It came down to her mid-thigh, so she was more than covered, but seeing her in his clothes hit him hard.

He wanted this woman.

The thought was so surprising, after being celibate for so long, that Willis couldn't speak.

Then he noticed something else. Something he hadn't seen earlier because she'd worn long pants and a long-sleeve shirt—the torn skin on her arm and leg. It looked painful as hell, and Willis winced. He hated to think how hard she'd hit the ground to abrade her skin through her clothes.

"Um...Princess needs to go outside. What are you doing up? Have you slept at all?"

Willis stood and walked over to Maylah. He wanted to ask if she was in pain. Wanted to pull her against his chest and keep her safe. But he forced himself to reach for the dog instead. "I'll take her," he said in a shaky voice.

"I can do it."

He shook his head. "It's dark out, and I don't

want to risk that whoever showed up at your house is out there watching."

"Oh," Maylah said nervously.

Willis wanted to kick himself. He hadn't meant to scare her. "It's okay. You're safe here," he reassured her.

"I...do you think he might come back? Are you in danger because I'm here?"

Willis stared at her for a beat. When was the last time anyone had worried about *his* safety? He couldn't remember. He was the big bad FBI agent with deadly connections. He was the man people turned to when they needed help.

Lifting a hand slowly, giving Maylah a chance to step away, Willis cradled her cheek. His thumb brushed against her in a feather-light caress. "You're sweet," he said softly.

She frowned. "No, I'm not," she protested.

Willis found himself smiling. He'd smiled more around this woman than he had since Elle died, period. "You foster abused and hurt animals. You're worried about a man you barely know. You're definitely sweet," he insisted.

He wasn't exactly surprised when Maylah continued to protest. "I'm a decent human being. Anyone would care about those things."

"You're wrong," Willis told her firmly. "For the

record? I like it." He could tell he'd surprised her. She stared up at him with wide eyes, confusion swimming in her gaze. He liked keeping her off-kilter. It was somewhat perverse of him, but he couldn't help it. Reaching out, Willis took Princess from her arms and was rewarded by the dog licking his hand.

He turned and headed for his back door. When he didn't spot anything out of the ordinary in the area, Willis put the dog on the ground and said, "Go on, do your business fast, Princess."

As if the dog understood, she immediately wandered a little way off and squatted. When she was done, she came right back to the door. Willis picked her up again and locked the door behind him. He turned—and almost ran into Maylah, who'd followed him without his knowledge.

It was surprising, because Willis was *always* aware of his surroundings. He had to be.

"How'd you know she wouldn't run?" Maylah asked.

Willis shrugged. "She knows she's got it good. She's not going to run off, not when there's the chance for more chicken and rice, and she's warm and safe here. Come on, it's still early, why don't you head back to bed and sleep for a little while longer?"

But Maylah shook her head. "I'm not tired." She ruined her firm statement with a huge yawn.

Willis smirked. "No?"

Maylah huffed out a breath. "Now that I'm not in as much pain and have gotten some rest, I can't sleep knowing I took your bed. And you're still in the same clothes you were in yesterday, minus the coat and tie. I feel guilty that you haven't slept at all."

Willis turned her by grasping her elbow. It almost physically hurt to drop his hand. "Come on," he said, gesturing back toward his living room.

She practically stomped in irritation as she went where he indicated, and Willis' smile grew. He liked her spunk. She twirled to face him when she entered the other room.

"How about if we hang out here?" he asked before she could say anything. "I'm expecting a few phone calls, but I could get some shut-eye while I'm waiting."

She eyed him skeptically. "Are you saying that just so I'll lay down again?"

"No. You're right. I'm tired. But I don't need a lot of sleep. If I can get a couple of hours, I'll be okay."

"That's not good for you," she said.

Willis felt his heart expand. There she went, worrying about him again. He had to admit it felt good. "Come on. You want water or anything?"

"No."

"Okay, you can have the recliner. I promise it's

comfy. I've fallen asleep in it more times than I can count. I'll take the couch." The sofa was easier to get out of in case he needed to defend Maylah from an intruder. But she didn't need to know that.

"Are you sure?"

"Positive," Willis told her.

She went over to his oversized suede recliner and gingerly sat. She scooted back and her feet dangled in front of her like a little kid sitting in an adult-size chair. She reached down and pulled on the handle on the side, sighing in contentment as the footrest came up and the chair reclined.

"Oh, this *is* comfy," she told him with a smile.

Willis grabbed a throw blanket from the couch. He spread it over her as best he could with one hand, and once she looked as snug as she could get, he gently placed Princess on her lap.

"You have another blanket for yourself, right?" she asked.

Willis had a feeling if he said no, she'd totally make him take the one he gave her back. So he quickly nodded. "Yes."

"Okay. Greg?"

"Yeah?"

"Thanks for letting me stay tonight. That guy rattled me more than I wanted to admit."

"You're welcome."

What Willis really wanted to say was that she could stay as long as she wanted, but he figured that would be a bit much this soon. It felt right having her in his space. His bed, his chair. He wasn't sure how to get her to *want* to stay. He didn't want her to agree solely because she was scared to go home. That wouldn't be the best start to a relationship.

He wasn't even surprised he was already thinking about a long-term relationship with this woman. She'd gotten under his skin immediately...and he liked her there.

Willis got settled on the couch, toeing his shoes off and leaning back against the cushions. He kept his gaze on Maylah and Princess. It didn't take long before they were both slightly snoring, the sound making him smile once more. He closed his eyes and sighed.

He might have messed up and lost his wife and daughter because he'd taken their safety for granted, but he wouldn't make that mistake again. He'd worked his ass off to protect women and children all over the world, and his neighbor was now his main focus. He'd find out who was behind her carjacking and make sure the man didn't even *think* about repeating his mistake.

CHAPTER FOUR

MAYLAH WATCHED GREG SLEEP. She'd woken up in his recliner and saw that he was fast asleep on the couch across from her. He looked just as put-together as he did when she saw him leaving for work in the mornings.

She could admit that she'd spied on her handsome neighbor more than once, peering through her curtains as he strode down his stairs to his car. He had an air of confidence that she admired. He was constantly aware of his surroundings. More than once, Maylah had seen him looking around when he first exited his brownstone, as if he was taking in the area, scanning it for threats. Of course, there weren't any. She'd picked this area of DC to live in because it was safe.

She also had to admit Greg Willis wasn't the kind

of man she was usually attracted to. He was average height and slender, wore suits almost every day, and looked as if he would be more at home behind a computer, rather than doing any kind of physical work.

But after only a few hours of being around him, Maylah realized that looks could be deceiving. Greg had an edge about him that made her think he was actually a bad boy in disguise. He might look like a nerd, but anyone around him for even a short length of time would discover he was anything but.

His hand on her arm made her want to lean on him. He was the kind of man who could make a woman feel protected. Who would give any man who dared catcall in her presence second thoughts about doing it twice.

The kind of man who wouldn't be able to walk away when he saw a woman struggling to get out of a cab after a very tough day.

And while she'd been terrified yesterday, she was completely relaxed now. Secure in the knowledge that she was protected in Greg's home. Even with him sound asleep, she felt more at ease than she'd been practically since Ted had died.

Ted had been her rock. Physically, he was a big man, tall and heavy. Muscular. Standing next to him had made her feel tiny, which she was. At five-five, she was shorter than average. But Ted would've made the tallest woman feel protected simply with his presence.

He'd also initiated more than one fistfight when he'd been drinking.

And while Greg seemed to be Ted's polar opposite, Maylah had no doubt that she was safe with him. He oozed competence...and an indefinably dangerous vibe that for some reason drew her like a moth to a flame, rather than repel her.

It made no sense, but Maylah didn't question it.

She was a big believer in fate. In finding the good in the bad. While she'd never wanted to experience the terror she felt when she'd been carjacked, she was here in her neighbor's space as a result. She'd been curious about Greg for quite a while now. He intrigued her, but she wasn't the kind of woman who pushed herself on others. And it was obvious her neighbor was a very busy man. He left early in the morning and came home late. It wasn't as if she could orchestrate accidental meetings that often. She'd done it a few times, going out to walk a foster around the time he usually left for work. But nothing had come of it but a few polite nods, and Maylah had started to feel like a stalker.

She smiled at the thought, considering she was watching Greg now. He was relaxed, and in sleep, when he let down his guard, he looked almost innocent.

A second later, the phone he gripped in his hand, even in sleep, rang out. It was fascinating to watch how he went from being knocked out to awake immediately.

"Willis," he said as he answered the phone.

Maylah had a moment to wonder how he managed not to sound completely groggy when woken from a sound sleep, before he sat up and exclaimed, "You have got to be shitting me!"

She sat up and lowered the footrest, immediately tensing at Greg's tone as he spoke to whoever was on the other end of the line.

"Oh, it's happening," Greg said harshly. "He's got a death wish. I assume you told him he's making a mistake. Right. Okay. I appreciate it."

He conversed with the caller for a few more minutes, then clicked off the connection without saying goodbye.

"Um...is everything all right?" Maylah asked.

"No." She watched as Greg swallowed hard and got himself under control. "Yes, sorry. It's fine."

"Don't do that," she said softly.

"Do what?" he asked, looking at her for the first time. His hair was mussed and if it was possible, he looked even more handsome than he had before.

"Sugarcoat whatever's upsetting you."

Greg stared at her for a long moment before nodding. "Sorry. Obviously, that wasn't good news," he said.

"About me?"

"Not directly. That was someone I know from the streets. I put out some feelers last night, and a confidential informant said the guy who took your car is afraid you got a good enough look at him that the cops will be able to ID him, which is partly why he came back to your house last night."

Maylah blinked in surprise. "You know who he is?"

"Me personally? No. I mean, I have a street name, but that's it."

"Then how can you know anything about him?"

"People talk," Greg said. "They can't help it. They want to boast about the shit they've done, or what they *plan* to do. That's how things work on the streets. The guy who stole your car was bragging about it to the wrong people, how he stole it in broad daylight. He's new to the area. Came up from Florida. Sounds like he wants to prove that he's a badass. But he doesn't know how things work around here."

Maylah waited for him to say more, but when he didn't, she asked, "How do things work?"

Willis smiled, but it wasn't the gentle expression

he'd offered last night. It was hard. "No one messes with me and mine. This guy hasn't learned that yet."

Maylah shivered. She supposed she should be offended by his words—or terrified. But instead, the thought of being his felt...*right*.

"Come on," he said, standing in front of her chair holding a hand out to her. Without a thought, she put her fingers in his and let him pull her upright.

"Princess, you're going to have to wait while we get ready. Here, you can have the chair until we're done," he told the little dog, taking her from Maylah's arm and placing her back down in the recliner. She immediately curled into a ball in the blanket that Maylah had been using and began snoring.

Greg hadn't let go of her hand, and he began walking toward the stairs. If it had been any other man, in any other situation, Maylah would've been stressing about where he was leading her and what would happen when they got there. But she trusted Greg. Implicitly and instinctually.

He took her back up to his bedroom, then turned to face her. His gaze ran down her body in a quick, assessing way, and when he met her eyes once more, she could see concern shining in his. "How're you feeling?"

"Pretty good, all things considered," she told him.

"Don't lie to me," he warned.

To her surprise, Maylah wasn't scared of his bossy attitude. "Seriously. It's amazing what a good meal and sleep can do."

His right hand came up and brushed against her bicep. It was a feather-light touch, so much so, she barely felt it. "You got torn up pretty good," he whispered as he stared at the scraped skin of her arm.

"You know, I didn't think twice about jumping out of the car," she told him. "Most normal people would struggle with that kind of decision. But I was moving before I even considered what I was doing. I think I instinctively knew that whatever happened when I hit the ground would be way better than whatever the guy had in store for me."

Greg inhaled deeply and his nostrils flared as his eyes shut, obviously getting his temper in line.

"I'm okay," Maylah said, wanting to soothe this man who'd done so much for her already. "Seriously," she insisted when he opened his eyes. "I'll be scabbed up and gross for a while, but I'll heal."

"Yeah," Greg whispered.

They stood like that for a while, staring at each other. Then Greg took a deep breath and dropped his hand. "The detective will be here in a little bit to talk to you about last night."

"Right," Maylah said.

"You want me to go to your place and get your shampoo and stuff?"

Maylah smiled. She had no doubt he'd do just that. "No. If it's okay, I can use what you have."

"It's definitely okay," Greg said. Then to her surprise, he smiled lazily. "You'll smell like me."

Without thought, Maylah retorted, "Does that mean if you shower at my place, you'll use my stuff and smell like *me*?"

The smile on Greg's face widened, but all he said was, "Take your time. If the detective gets here before you're ready, he can wait." Then he went to a dresser against the wall and crouched on the balls of his feet to open the bottom drawer. When he stood, he was holding something pink. And he suddenly looked hesitant. "As much as I like you in my shirt, it's a little big. You'd probably be more comfortable in this." He looked apprehensive as he held the clothes out to her.

Holding them up, Maylah saw they were a woman's shirt and a pair of sweatpants.

"They were my wife's. She loved being comfortable. As soon as she got home at night, she changed into sweats and a comfy shirt. Those might still be a little big, but that's probably not a bad thing with the road rash you've got."

Maylah stared at him, all sorts of feelings rolling

through her. Finally, she blurted, "You don't mind me wearing her things?"

Greg shook his head. "I think she would've insisted on sharing her clothes with you if she was here, actually. I don't have a lot of her stuff. I don't even know why I kept *those*... No, that's not true. I do. It took me two years to even start giving away Elle and Molly's things. But I kept some of their clothes. Not much, but...it was a comfort at the time. If it's too weird, again, I can go over to your place and grab something for you to wear."

"No, it's fine...as long as it won't bother you to see me in her clothes."

Greg brought his hand up once more and palmed the side of her face. His touch sent electricity shooting down to her toes. Maylah leaned her head into his hand. "It doesn't bother me," he reassured her. "I loved Elle more than anything in the world. But she's gone. She'd want me to open myself up to someone else again."

"Is that what you're doing?" Maylah asked quietly.

"I must not be doing it right if you have to ask," he said dryly.

"You are," Maylah said quickly. "Doing it right, that is."

"Good," Greg whispered.

They stood like that for a long moment, his hand

on her cheek, her leaning against him. Then he took a deep breath, and his thumb caressed her cheek once before he stepped back. "If you need anything, just let me know and I'll get it for you."

She had no doubt of that. "Okay," she said softly.

Greg backed away, not taking his gaze from hers. Then he took another deep breath and returned to the dresser where he'd gotten the clothes for her. He opened a couple drawers, and carried an armful of clothes with him when he headed for the bedroom door.

He left without another word, shutting the door behind him firmly.

Maylah let out the breath she hadn't realized she'd been holding when he was gone. Greg was intense...in a good way.

It was still hard to believe she was here, in her neighbor's bedroom, about to get naked and shower in his bathroom. She'd watched him from the safety of her home for what seemed like forever. She'd admired him from afar...and had a crush on him for almost as long. A secret crush on a man she didn't even know.

As she looked down at the clothes, tears unexpectedly sprang to her eyes. "I'll take care of him," she whispered, then headed for the bathroom.

CHAPTER FIVE

MAYLAH COULDN'T KEEP her gaze from Greg. She'd never seen him in anything but the dark suits he always wore. But when she'd come downstairs after showering and changing into the clothes he'd given her, she'd almost screamed when she glimpsed the stranger in his living room.

But it wasn't a stranger, of course. It was Greg. He had on a pair of jeans and a T-shirt, and if she thought he was handsome in his suit and tie, he was even more gorgeous like this. He looked more approachable, more...vulnerable. She suddenly realized that he used his formal attire as another form of armor. To keep people at arm's length.

When she'd commented that she'd never seen him in jeans before, he seemed uncomfortable and self-conscious. So she'd dropped it...but she still couldn't take her eyes off him.

He'd made them breakfast, and even Princess got some of the eggs and bacon. Then, despite her objections, he went over to her place to grab the painkillers she'd been prescribed. When he gave her a key to her new lock, Maylah had been shocked. She couldn't believe he'd found someone to change her locks in the middle of the night.

When there was a knock at his door an hour after they'd eaten, Maylah jerked in fright.

"It's okay, it's the detective," Greg soothed. But he didn't get up to let him in.

Maylah nodded, but when he still didn't move, she asked, "Are you going to let him in?"

"Do you feel comfortable talking to him right now?"

She frowned. "Does that matter?" she asked.

"Of course."

"What happens if I say no?"

"Then I'll tell him to come back later."

"That would be rude," Maylah whispered.

Greg simply shrugged. "Don't care. You aren't ready, you don't have to talk to him."

This guy.

"It's okay, I'm ready."

"Are you sure?"

"Yeah. The sooner I talk to him, the sooner he'll hopefully find the guy who stole my car—and hopefully my car too—and the sooner I can get out of your hair."

Another knock sounded at the door, but Greg still didn't look as though he was remotely interested in answering. His entire focus was on her. "*I'm* going to find him," he said firmly. "And you aren't in my hair...not in a bad way, that is."

Maylah swallowed hard at the thought of staying right where she was, in Greg's comfy chair, Princess on her lap, being treated as if she was the most important person in the world. "How are you going to find him?" she asked.

"He threatened you. Made you jump out of a moving car. Hurt you. Trust me—I'll find him." Then Greg finally stood from the sofa and headed for the door.

Having a break from his intensity was a good thing. Maylah took a deep breath and tried to regain her composure. She didn't understand how or why she and Greg seemed to connect so quickly, but she wasn't complaining. It just took a little getting used to. She'd kind of retreated behind the walls of her home after Ted died. The money from his life insurance and investments was enough to afford her a simple lifestyle, and she didn't need to get a job. So she'd taken a step back from everyone and everything and thrown herself into taking care of the animals who needed her.

Being the subject of Greg's attention was both disconcerting and a dream come true.

"Hello, Ms. Brant. I'm sorry we have to meet again so soon," Detective Greer said as he entered the room.

She got up from the recliner and walked toward him. She'd talked to the detective at the hospital and had given him as much information as she could about her carjacking.

"Do you have any leads?" she asked nervously.

"Not yet, but we'll get him," the detective told her. "Is there anything else you can tell us about him? Maybe something you hadn't remembered in the hospital?"

Maylah's gaze flicked to Greg, and he gave her a small shake of his head right before he asked the detective, "Would you like something to drink?"

While the officer turned to Greg, Maylah tried to interpret the look Greg had given her. She thought about his call with someone he'd called a confidential informant. She was *sure* he'd gotten some information about who might've stolen her car and who had come into her home the night before—because before hanging up, he'd told whoever was on the other end of the line to "hold on to Zero" if they found him.

It seemed clear to her that he didn't want her telling the detective about that conversation, or mentioning the name Zero. If it had been anyone else —anyone other than her neighbor who seemed to have a lot more layers to him than anyone knew—she wouldn't have a problem telling Detective Greer everything. But she trusted Greg.

They all sat at the small table just off the kitchen, and Maylah listened to the detective explain what he and other officers were doing to track down her carjacker. How they had a BOLO out for her car, and he had high hopes it would be found and returned. How they were talking with people on the streets about the incident and searching for surveillance footage that might give them a better view of the man who'd taken her hostage while stealing her car.

"Why do you think the man who came into your apartment was the same one who stole your vehicle?"

Maylah stared at him with what she knew had to be an incredulous look on her face. "You *don't* think it was him?" she asked.

"Well, yeah, I do, but I was wondering if you were one hundred percent sure it was the same guy."

"I don't know who else it *could* be," Maylah said.

The detective stared at her for a moment before asking, "Are you dating?"

Maylah stiffened. She didn't know what that had to do with anything. "No," she said, even though the word felt weird after sleeping in Greg's bed, wearing his dead wife's clothes, and using his body soap in the shower that morning.

"Could it have been an ex-boyfriend who you gave a key to?" the detective pressed.

"I haven't dated anyone since my husband died," she told him.

She hated the look of skepticism on the man's face. She understood that he was used to dealing with people who lied. Probably about everything. But she wasn't one of them, and it was frustrating that he didn't believe her.

"You know as well as we do that her purse was in the car," Greg said in a low tone—that was all the more scary for the control he was showing. "And inside her purse was her ID with her address on it. It doesn't take a rocket scientist to realize the person who walked into her house, after unlocking her door with *her own key*, was the asshole who kidnapped her and forced her to jump out of a moving car. Why don't we move on to more productive questions."

It wasn't a request.

"Right. Can you describe him for me again?"

Maylah squeezed her hands together in her lap under the table. She hadn't been half this stressed when the detective had interviewed her in the hospital. Probably thanks to the painkillers. But today, once again, it felt like he didn't believe her. And that sucked. "I told you what I could remember about him yesterday."

"Yes, but do you remember anything else after seeing him last night?"

"He had on a mask," Maylah admitted.

The look of frustration on Detective Greer's face made her feel as if she'd answered the question wrong in front of the entire class. "The knife looked the same," she blurted.

"The same as what?" It was Greg who asked.

Maylah looked over at him. She much preferred his look of patience and anger toward the man who dared break into her house, over the skeptical look on the detective's face. "He had a gun when he told me to get in my car," she said. "He pointed it at my head, and I had the feeling he would've shot me without a second thought if I didn't do what he said. So I got in and climbed over to the passenger seat. After he got into the car and started driving, he reached down and pulled out a knife from some kind of holster thing at his side. He held it in his right hand, and the gun in the left, as he drove. He pointed the knife at me and told me he was going to use it to carve his name into my flesh. That he was going to—" Her voice hitched, then lowered to a shaky whisper as she continued, "To stick it up inside me after he fucked me."

The anger that flared in Greg's eyes was instantaneous. "He *what*?" he demanded.

"It's why I jumped," Maylah said. "I couldn't... No matter how many bones I broke jumping, it was better than...that," she said.

"How do you know it was the same knife?" Detective Greer asked.

But Maylah couldn't take her eyes off Greg. His jaw was ticking and it looked as if he was about to lose his shit right then and there. Without thought, she reached over and put a hand over one of his that was fisted in his lap. "It's okay. It didn't happen," she said gently.

"Ms. Brant? The knife?" the detective pushed.

Greg unclenched his hand under hers and twisted his wrist, interlacing his fingers with hers almost desperately. Whatever was happening between them was happening at lightning speed. And it felt right.

She brought her gaze back to the officer. "There was a design on the knife itself. Flowers etched into the blade. I saw them in the car, and I saw them again last night."

"I thought you said you were across the room from him," Detective Greer pressed.

"I was. But the light from the living room glinted off the blade."

The officer pressed his lips together. It was obvious he didn't actually believe she'd notice such a small detail. He asked a few more questions, but they were things she'd already told him the day before. He expressed skepticism that the carjacker would be stupid enough to come to her house hours after he'd stolen her car.

Eventually, he left, promising her and Greg that he'd be in touch.

The second the door shut behind the detective, Greg began to pace in agitation. He ran a hand through his hair and mumbled under his breath.

"Greg?" she asked from her spot near the table, where she'd remained after shaking the detective's hand.

In response, Greg stalked toward her. He reached out and took her head in his hands. "He's not going to touch you. Understand?"

Maylah reached up and grabbed his wrists as she nodded.

"I mean it. This asshole isn't going to get within ten feet of you again. I won't allow it."

She needed to calm him. A vein in his forehead

was bulging and his grip on either side of her head was almost painful. Then she remembered what she'd read when she'd given into her curiosity one night and typed his name into a search engine online.

His wife and daughter had been raped by their kidnappers before they'd been murdered.

"Greg. I trust you. You'll keep me safe," she murmured, running her hands up and down his forearms slowly.

"Damn straight I will," he said between clenched teeth. Then he took a deep breath, and wrapped an arm around her waist and pulled her into him. His head dropped to the space between her shoulder and neck as he held her close.

They stood like that for a minute or two, before Maylah said, "Couch."

"What?" he mumbled without lifting his head.

"Let's go sit," she told him. "On the couch."

He escorted her over, still holding her against him, until they were sitting. He shifted her to straddle his waist, and she melted against his chest. "Is this hurting your leg?" he asked into her neck.

"No."

Bit by bit, Maylah felt his muscles begin to relax under her. "Tell me about them?"

Immediately after the words left her mouth, she

tensed. She didn't want to pry, and he'd finally relaxed. But he didn't tense up with her.

"I will...if you'll tell me about Ted."

"Okay." Surprisingly, Maylah found she was eager to tell Greg about her husband. She hadn't had anyone to talk to about him in a very long time. Her own parents were dead, and after Ted passed, his parents kind of just faded away. She'd tried to maintain a connection, but without Ted, they didn't seem interested.

She felt Greg take a deep breath, then he began to speak.

CHAPTER SIX

"I MET ELLE AT WORK," Willis started, the words flowing out of him without thought. He didn't like to talk about his wife and daughter. It hurt too much. But somehow, with Maylah cuddled up against him, it didn't hurt as badly as it always had in the past.

"I didn't think she noticed me at all. She was beautiful, and I was...well...me. Nerdy, too focused on work, kind of grumpy. She was an administrative assistant to one of the bigwigs at the FBI office, and was in the break room one day. She dropped a bottle of pickles and glass and juice went everywhere. She was wearing open-toe sandals, and I didn't think, I simply picked her up, carrying her away from the broken glass and the mess. That didn't help my cause. We didn't click immediately. She thought I was arrogant and presumptuous. But eventually I wore her down and she said yes when I asked if she wanted to go out to lunch.

"We dated for three years before she agreed to marry me. Molly was conceived within a few months of us being married. I loved them so much...but I was stupid. Too worried about moving up in the organization. I missed a lot of Molly's dance recitals, too many dinners with my family, and we rarely took vacations together because I was too consumed with work. Elle quit her job to be a full-time mother, and while she loved it, I think she also missed being appreciated."

"I'm sure you appreciated her," Maylah murmured.

Her head was resting on his shoulder and one hand was at his nape, caressing gently. Goose bumps had sprouted on his arms from her touch...and weren't retreating.

Willis felt guilty for feeling so *energized* by her touch. Had he ever felt like this when Elle touched him? If so, he didn't remember.

"I *did* appreciate her," Willis said with a sigh. "But I didn't tell her nearly enough. I took her for granted. She was always there for Molly. To kiss boo-boos, to make her lunches and dinner, drive her to her extracurricular activities, and to cheer her on in whatever she was doing. When I had to go to France, I had the great idea to take Elle and Molly with me. I'm not sure either really wanted to go, but they didn't want to disappoint me. Molly had to miss a school dance and was grumpy about it, as many teenage girls would be. Still, I hoped that being in France would help cheer them up.

"But of course when we got there, they were pretty much on their own, as usual. I was too busy tracking down a suspected spy who'd fled to the city. I threw money at them and told them to go shopping. I should've gone with them," Willis said desolately.

"You couldn't have known," Maylah soothed, sitting up and trying to catch his eye.

"I wasn't there when they needed me most," Willis said, closing his eyes, not wanting her to see the shame in his gaze. His soul. "They were kidnapped, abused in the worst way, and I couldn't find them. I'd spent my entire career tracking down bad guys—and I couldn't find them!" His voice cracked. He took a deep breath and forced himself to look at the woman on his lap. He didn't deserve her, he knew that, but he couldn't make himself release his tight hold.

To Willis' surprise, he didn't see condemnation in her gaze. He saw sorrow and understanding.

"You *were* there. You were here," she said, putting

her hand over his heart. "They knew you were looking for them. That you wouldn't stop until you found them. That certainty kept them going right to the end."

Willis swallowed hard, but it didn't stop the sob from escaping his throat.

Maylah lay back down on his chest and squeezed him tightly. He held on with an almost desperate grip. "I loved them. So much," he whispered into her hair.

"I know you did."

"They didn't deserve that."

"No, they didn't," Maylah soothed.

Surprisingly, it didn't take long for Willis to gain control over himself once more. Usually when he let himself think about his lost family, he got sucked down into a pit of despair that took several hours to shake out of. But with Maylah in his arms, with her understanding and support, he was able to breathe normally far faster than usual.

"Can you tell me about your husband?" he asked.

Maylah nodded against him, but didn't lift her head. "He was awesome. Big, protective...a guy's guy. He loved sports, drinking beer, hanging out with his friends. He loved meat and potatoes and didn't like working out much. He worked hard and partied hard."

"You aren't a partier," Willis said.

"No. But even though we were different, we worked," Maylah told him. "I was happy to stay at home—I'm not super social—while he went out with his friends. I always waited up for him to get home.

"The night before...he'd stayed out later than usual. He didn't get home until around two in the morning. He was drunk, but a happy drunk. He got up in the morning at his normal time. He was grumpy, but I wasn't surprised since I figured he was still hungover. I stayed in bed while he got up to get ready for work. He showered, got dressed, kissed me goodbye, then went downstairs. I fell back asleep, since I had been up so late waiting for him, and woke a couple hours later.

"I went downstairs...and couldn't understand what I was seeing. Ted was on the kitchen floor, and I had the stupid thought that he'd decided to take a nap or something. It wasn't until I walked closer that I saw his eyes were open and he was staring up at the ceiling. When I touched him, he was cold. He was gone. Probably had the heart attack right after he'd gone down the stairs. He hadn't even started his coffee yet. If I hadn't gone back to sleep, maybe I would've heard him fall. I could've called for help and he would still be alive."

Willis shook his head. "His death wasn't your fault."

Maylah shrugged. "Maybe. Maybe not."

They were both silent for a while. Then Willis said, "For a long time, I didn't think it was possible to get involved with anyone again. It felt as if I would be cheating on Elle and Molly. But now..." His voice faded.

"Now?" Maylah asked.

"Now I think maybe I could. I learned my lesson with Elle. I'll never take someone I love for granted again. I'll make sure I'm home for dinner. I'll give her my full attention. I'll make sure she never has one second of doubt about my feelings for her."

"I'm sure Elle knew you loved her," Maylah told him.

"Yeah, but I know in my heart I wasn't the partner she deserved," Willis said with a shrug. "I wasn't the father Molly deserved either. My chance to be a father is long gone, but I will never let anyone I'm in a relationship with ever doubt that she's the most important person in my life. That she's more important than work."

Willis stared at Maylah, a pang of longing sweeping through him as he looked into her eyes. He needed her to hear him. To know that if she was that woman, *his* woman, he wouldn't let her down as he'd done to Elle and his daughter.

"Greg," she whispered.

Moving slowly, giving her time to pull back, Willis leaned forward.

Not only did she not pull back, she met him halfway. Her hand at his nape tightened as she pressed her lips to his. Their kiss was slow and sweet to start with. Then she pulled back and licked her lips as she stared at him, breathing hard.

Without thought, Willis moved. He cradled her head in his hand as he eased her back on the couch, shifting until she was lying under him.

"I'm going to find him," he vowed, needing her to trust him.

"Okay."

"I mean it. I haven't spent decades hobnobbing with the worst of the worst, cultivating dubious relationships for information, staining my soul by looking the other way when people break the law, only to let this asshole get away with what he's done. With threatening you."

"I said okay, Greg," Maylah reassured him.

"I'm gray," he warned her. "I've overlooked drug deals, robberies, illegal gun sales, all in order to get to the highest man on the totem pole. I've authorized teams around the country to kill people. I've celebrated the deaths of men and women across the globe who've taken women, children, and men hostage. I'm not a good man, Maylah. I need you to know this."

To his surprise, she laughed. Threw her head back and actually *guffawed*.

When she had herself under control, she lifted a hand and speared her fingers into his hair. "Not a good man? Greg, you're one of the best men I've had the honor of knowing. If you think I'm going to care that you organized the deaths of people who've *kidnapped* people, you're wrong. You've taken what happened to your family and turned it into something good. No, that's not the right word... Righteous, maybe."

Willis realized he was breathing hard. His heart was beating almost out of his chest, and his fingers itched to tear this woman's clothes off and show her without words just how much her trust and belief in him meant. But he controlled himself. Barely.

"So we're doing this?" he asked gruffly.

"If by this, you mean having sex...yes," she said with a shy smile.

"No, I mean *this*...an exclusive relationship. Living together. Waking up and going to bed together. Respecting each other, getting married, getting old, vacationing."

She blinked up at him in surprise. Then she

shocked the shit out of him by nodding. "I think we are."

"Don't agree until you're sure," Willis warned.

Maylah chuckled. "If you think I've missed how intense you are, I haven't," she told him. "But you might decide you want someone who enjoys going out. Who can easily have conversations with strangers. Who's happy going to work functions rather than staying home behind closed doors."

"I won't," he told her. "But I can't stop working," he warned. "There are too many people out there who need finding. Rescuing."

"I'd never ask you to do that," Maylah said gently.

"How do your scrapes feel? Your head?" Willis asked.

Maylah frowned up at him. "They're okay. Why?"

"Because I need you, Maylah. I need to make you mine." Willis was aware he was moving too fast. That it was very likely Maylah was enamored with him solely because she was grateful he was there last night when that man broke into her house. But it was a chance he was willing to take. Having this woman even once would be better than never having her at all.

"This is crazy," she breathed.

Willis nodded, not surprised she was thinking the

same thing he was. But the next words out of her mouth weren't what he was expecting to hear.

"I don't want you to regret this. When I love, I love hard," she said, as if that was a bad thing. "I can be clingy, you'll probably get annoyed with how much I try to take care of you. How I won't be able to sleep until you get home. How I insist on getting up at the same time as you in the morning to make you breakfast and to see you off to work."

He knew that came from what happened to her husband. "I won't," he said without a shred of doubt.

She stared at him for a moment. "We're moving too fast." But she didn't sound too worried about that.

"Yes," he agreed.

"But I feel as if I've known you forever," she whispered. "That I've simply been treading water in my life, waiting for you to come into it."

"Same," Willis agreed. And he did. This woman had seeped into his soul without any effort whatsoever. It was weird. And so damn right.

"I don't think I told you, but you're extremely handsome in your suit and tie. I spent many mornings and evenings watching you come and go from your place. But in this T-shirt and jeans? You're *irresistible*."

"I'm nothing like what you said your husband looked like," Willis said a little self-consciously.

"No, you aren't," she agreed. "But I can tell you this, I've never been more desperate to see what a man looks like under his clothes than I am you."

He grinned. "Yeah?"

"Yeah," she said with a nod.

"Just remember that I spend most of my time behind a computer, not working out."

"And I spend most of *my* time in my house, cooking, eating, and taking care of foster animals."

"And you're perfect," Willis said, his fingers itching to touch her. But he wouldn't do a damn thing without her permission and consent.

When she smiled and moved her hands to his waist, then under his shirt and up his chest, Willis broke. He straightened to his knees and tore his shirt over his head. He needed her hands on him. Touching him all over.

Maylah sighed under him and her gaze immediately went to his chest, where her hands began to caress him.

His nipples tightened and his cock hardened in his jeans. It had been so long since he'd had an erection, it actually startled Willis for a moment. Then he stood, ignoring her whimper of protest, and leaned over to pick her up off the couch.

She didn't ask where he was taking her, she simply snuggled into his grip as he once again headed up the stairs. There were phone calls Willis needed to take care of. A cocky asshole to track down. A point he needed to make. But at the moment, all he could think about was making this woman feel good. Making sure she didn't regret giving herself to him. Because that's what she was doing.

From here on out, she was his. To protect. To pamper. To love.

He'd loved Elle, but what he was feeling for Maylah felt bigger. Wilder. Out of his control.

He lay her down on his bed as if she was a precious piece of glass and stood there staring at her for a beat, not sure what he'd done in his life to deserve this second chance.

"Come here," Maylah whispered, holding up an arm as she reached for him.

He couldn't resist her. He was done trying to be noble.

CHAPTER SEVEN

MAYLAH HELD her breath as Greg stared down at her. Then he moved quickly, bracing himself over her. He lowered his head and she met him halfway once again. She couldn't resist him. It was as if everything within her was calling out for him. Urging her to make this man her own.

Their tongues swirled together almost desperately. She dug her nails into the back of his neck, holding him against her, urging him to give more of himself.

"Easy, little one, I'm here," he murmured.

Ted had never given her a nickname. Maylah hadn't minded, hadn't even noticed. But every cell in her body sat up and took notice when Greg called her "little one." He sat up and his fingers went to the buttons on the shirt she'd put on that morning. Slowly easing each one out of the hole, baring her body inch by inch.

She had a moment of uncertainty as he spread the shirt open, exposing her chest to him. She hadn't lied —she didn't go out much, didn't like working out, cooked when she was bored, and ended up eating most of what she made. She also wasn't exactly young anymore. Would he like what he saw? Would he be as turned on by looking at her as she was by seeing him without a shirt?

The answer was apparently yes, if his sharp inhalation and the look of lust blooming in his eyes was any indication.

"So damn beautiful," he breathed, before leaning down and nuzzling the cleavage between her breasts, exposed by the sports bra she had on. It wasn't the sexiest of undergarments, but he didn't seem to care in the least.

He sat up, licked his lips, then eased the shirt off her shoulders. Arching her back, Maylah helped him pull the material out from under her. She expected him to touch her then. To palm her breasts, or even to push the sweatpants over her hips. But instead, he surprised her by leaning over and brushing his lips over the injured flesh on her right arm. He kissed his way down her arm with feather-light kisses, as if the touch of his lips could heal her.

Maylah's eyes filled with tears. She'd missed this. Missed feeling as if she was the most important woman in her partner's eyes. Ted was a good husband, but he hadn't been the most romantic of men. They hadn't spent a lot of time caressing and cuddling in bed. He was as focused about sex as he was everything else in his life. She hadn't realized what she'd been missing...until now.

"Greg," she whispered, feeling overwhelmed.

"Did I hurt you?" he asked, lifting his head, looking concerned.

"No." She rushed to reassure him. "Not even close."

He nodded, then his mouth was moving over her torso, leaving little kisses along every inch of skin as he went. Her entire body felt energized by the time he lifted himself over her once again. "How do we get this off without hurting you?" he asked as he fingered the tight band of her bra across her rib cage.

Maylah sat up, and Greg immediately scooted back, giving her room. She lifted her arms over her head. "Up and off," she told him.

He smiled and nodded as he gripped the elastic at the bottom of her bra. His eyes went to her chest as he lifted the tight material over her breasts. The look of lust she saw once more blooming in his gaze made her feel ten times more confident than she'd been before.

Once again, his control was impressive. He didn't immediately grab for her, didn't shove her on her back and lunge. He carefully lifted her bra up and over her hands before throwing the material off to the side of the bed. Then his hands ran down her arms slowly, making goose bumps break out all over her body. When he reached her shoulders, she lay back down with a sigh.

A small smile formed on his lips before his hands slowly—ever so slowly—moved toward her chest. Arching her back to urge him on, Maylah sighed when his palms finally closed over her breasts. Her nipples immediately tightened as he squeezed lightly.

Then his head lowered as he crouched over her. His lips closed over one of her nipples and an involuntary moan escaped her throat. That made him lift his head immediately. "Okay?" he asked.

"Yes! Please, yes..." she said breathily.

The smile returned as he resumed his attention on her nipple. His hands squeezed and massaged as he went from one nipple to the other. Maylah was a pile of mush by the time he lifted his lips from her skin.

"More?" he asked.

"More," she said firmly.

His hands went to the waistband of her sweats...finally.

Maylah lifted her hips to assist and, to her surprise, Greg pulled her underwear off with the sweats. She lay before him completely naked, but didn't have time to feel self-conscious, because he immediately dropped down between her legs and shoved her thighs apart roughly. In contrast, his head moved down and he nuzzled her inner thigh gently.

When he didn't do anything else, she lifted her head and asked, "Greg?"

"Shhhhh," he whispered. "I'm memorizing this moment."

Maylah bit her lip and let her head drop down to the pillow. "Right, I'll just be up here...waiting."

She felt more than heard his huff of laughter. Then he began exploring. He ran a finger between her folds, and Maylah would've been embarrassed at how wet she already was if he hadn't groaned low in his throat in reverence.

Jerking when he touched her clit, Maylah let out the breath she was holding.

"Oh, yeah," he said, more to himself than her. "There she is." Then he began to rub her clit with his thumb as he licked between her folds.

It was overwhelming, and for a moment she tried to pull away.

Of course Greg noticed. He immediately stilled and lifted his head. "Maylah? Is this okay?" he asked.

She nodded. "I just...it's been a while. And Ted didn't...um... Yeah, it's okay." She bit her lip, not knowing if Greg would be turned off or mad that she'd mentioned her husband.

"I love going down on a woman," Greg said softly. "Elle wasn't comfortable with it, so I rarely got the chance."

Maylah sighed in relief. He didn't sound upset, and she wasn't freaked out by him mentioning his wife either. "Well, I don't know if I like this, since I don't have the experience. So...why don't you do your thing and we'll see?"

He grinned up at her, and Maylah was amazed at how relaxed and happy he looked. "You're going to love it," he said cockily, and Maylah had a feeling he was right. Even now, with only a few touches, she felt tingles shooting from between her legs and she craved more.

Even in the midst of his excitement and lust, Greg was very gentle with her leg, careful not to rub against the scraped skin. This man was completely in tune with her, and yet again, she was momentarily overwhelmed.

Then all thoughts flew from her mind as Greg's lips latched onto her clit.

She jerked in his grip and her hands reached down to tangle in his hair. She felt as if she was flying apart, and the only thing holding her together was her grip on Greg.

The man was *very* good at this. Maylah couldn't understand why anyone wouldn't love what he was doing. This was ten times better than any sex she'd ever had, and he wasn't even inside her yet.

Greg took his time, nipping, licking, sucking. When he brought a hand between her legs and sank a finger slowly into her body Maylah couldn't hold back a small squeak.

"You're so wet. So hot," Greg murmured as he lifted his head.

Looking down her body, Maylah saw his gaze fixed on his finger, which he was pushing in and out of her body. Her belly clenched at the erotic sight. Then he looked up, and every nerve ending in Maylah's body tingled. She'd loved Ted, and he loved her back. But he'd never looked at her like Greg was right this moment. As if she was the most beautiful, precious, important person in the world. As if what he was doing meant the world to him.

Greg leaned down and reverently kissed the crease where her leg met her torso.

"Please," she whispered.

"Please what?" Greg asked with a small smile.

Maylah was aware he was teasing her, but she didn't care. She also didn't feel awkward telling him exactly what she wanted. Nothing felt more natural, more right, than being with this man.

"I want you inside me. I need you."

The teasing look in his expression morphed into lust. He immediately came up onto his knees and reached for the fastening of his jeans. He popped the button and without fanfare, jerked the material over his hips. He shifted to the side and kicked them off one leg, then the other.

When he straightened, he was as naked as she was, and Maylah eagerly looked her fill. His cock was hard, long, and dripping with precome.

Maylah couldn't help but lick her lips in anticipation. She was somewhat relieved he wasn't super thick. Without thought, a hand lifted from where she'd rested it on his thigh and moved toward his cock. She circled him, then caressed him from the base to the tip and back down.

Greg's head fell back, and Maylah loved the sway she held over this man right then. She had a feeling he didn't let his control slip much, but the groan that left his lips made her feel extremely powerful. She continued to stroke him until he reached his limit. He grabbed her hand and lifted it off his cock before leaning over her.

He stared down at her for a long moment. Finally, he said, "Be sure."

"I'm sure," Maylah said with no hesitation whatsoever. She wanted this man. All of him. She'd been fascinated with her neighbor for years, and being here right now...it was a fantasy come true.

"Birth control?" he asked tightly.

Maylah smiled. "I'm way past the desire or ability to have kids," she told him with a small laugh.

"You aren't that old," he said.

"Forty-eight. And while I know some women are able to conceive later than that, I'm on the pill to regulate my periods. I appreciate you asking though."

"Always. And...you're the first woman I've been with since Elle," Greg said solemnly.

"Same. I mean, since my husband died," Maylah said, feeling shy all of a sudden.

He smiled at her and brushed a lock of hair off her forehead. "It's never felt like this," he admitted. "I loved my wife, but this is...it's overwhelming."

"Yes," Maylah breathed.

"We don't have to—"

"Yes, we do!" she quickly countered.

Greg smiled down at her. "Thank God we're on the same page. I'll go slow."

Maylah nodded.

Then he moved a hand down between them, and she felt the head of his cock brush against her folds. She widened her legs and held her breath.

———

It was taking every ounce of Willis' control not to shove himself so deeply inside this woman, she'd never remember a time when he wasn't a part of her. But the last thing he wanted was to hurt her.

His teeth clenched when he notched the head of his cock between her folds. She was wet and hot, and she'd tasted like heaven when he'd gone down on her. He could've feasted on her all night and been perfectly happy. There was nothing like getting a woman off with his fingers and tongue. But when she'd begged for him to enter her, he hadn't been strong enough to resist.

When she made a small sound in the back of her throat, Willis immediately paused.

Not even half of his cock was inside her yet, but he couldn't mistake the small movement of her hips away from him.

"Easy, little one. I'm not going to hurt you." Willis

shifted so he could get a hand between their bodies and began to stroke her clit. He felt her inner muscles clench him, and once again he wanted nothing more than to thrust all the way inside her, but he held himself still as he did his best to stimulate Maylah.

Little by little, her inner muscles relaxed, but he waited until her hips thrust up against him before slowly moving once more.

They both groaned when he was all the way inside her, when their pubic hair meshed together. Then he brought a hand to her ass, and squeezed, pushing inside her a millimeter farther.

"You're so deep," she said between pants.

"Too much?" Willis asked.

"No!" she said with an almost violent shake of her head. "It feels amazing."

"Good," he said with satisfaction. "I'm not hurting you?"

Maylah shook her head. "No. For a moment there it pinched, but now it's good."

"Only good?" he asked with a grin. "That's not acceptable."

She grinned up at him. "Move, Greg. Please."

"So polite," he teased. "Let's see if I can make you a little more demanding." Then he began to thrust, slow and steady. He pulled almost all the way out of her, until just the head of his cock was inside, then paused.

"*Greg*," she whined, and he grinned.

To his amazement, Willis realized he was having fun. Sex had always been a serious thing for him in the past. He moved his hips forward until he was buried all the way inside Maylah once again. He continued with the slow and steady pace until he felt her fingers dig into his arms.

"Harder, Greg. Please!"

She was extremely slick now, able to take him without any issue. All Willis wanted to do was hammer inside her until he filled her to the brim, but she hadn't orgasmed yet. Which was unacceptable.

He grabbed hold of her hips and rested back on his heels. She made a little gasp of surprise as he manhandled her, but didn't protest. He spread his legs a little, making sure his cock stayed lodged inside her, but in this position he had his hands free, didn't need to hold himself above her.

Her legs were spread to accommodate his waist, and the sight of her pussy stretched around his cock was more erotic than anything he'd ever seen.

It was hard to believe this was happening. He'd watched his little neighbor more than he was comfortable admitting. He'd even jerked off to the thought of having her in exactly this position.

And now she was.

One hand went between her legs and the other reached up to pinch one of her nipples. Once again, she jerked in his grip, arching into his touch.

"So beautiful," he murmured.

Willis concentrated on learning what she liked...a fairly hard pinch on her nipple and a strong, steady touch on her clit. It wasn't long before she was writhing in his grip and he had to put a hand on her hip to hold her in place. A light sheen of sweat formed on her forehead and when she stared at up at him, it felt even more intimate than before.

"Come for me," he urged. "I want to feel you cream on my cock. Want to feel it dripping out of you."

"Greg!" she gasped as her fingernails dug into the skin of his forearm. But she wasn't pulling his hand away from between her legs, she was pushing into his touch, begging for more. So he gave her more.

His thumb pressed against her clit harder, and he moved it faster. She was humping against him so hard, his cock sliding only ever so slightly in and out of her channel. It was carnal and erotic, and Willis was so ready, he knew it wouldn't take much for him to explode.

When she finally did fly over the edge, her body squeezed his cock so hard it was almost painful. He moved even before her body stopped shaking. Had her flush with the bed, hovering over her, being careful not to touch the scrapes on her thigh. His hips snapped forward and back, Maylah keening as she grabbed him and held on while he powered in and out of her. Their skin slapped together as their bodies met, and the sound of his cock thrusting into her soaked pussy was loud in the otherwise quiet room.

Willis' balls tingled as his orgasm approached.

"Yes, Greg. Harder!" Maylah begged as she lifted her hips into each of his thrusts.

She was more than he'd expected, more than he deserved. He pushed into her as far as he could go, then lifted slightly and once again began to strum her clit. Maylah squealed under him and immediately began coming once more.

It was then and only then that Willis allowed himself to let go.

He came so hard, his head spun. He panted as he emptied himself deep inside her still rippling sheath. He couldn't remember ever being torn this inside out from an orgasm before. It was almost painful in its intensity.

His arms shook and he fell on top of Maylah. He managed not to completely squish her, burying his nose into her hair as he attempted to catch his breath.

"Holy crap," she murmured as her hands roamed up and down his back.

Willis lifted his head and stared at her for a moment before kissing her. It wasn't an easy kiss. It was hard, deep, and passionate. He told her without words how much what they'd just done meant to him.

When he pulled back, they were both breathing hard once more. Willis' cock had softened after the monster orgasm, but he was never so glad for his length, because it meant that he could stay inside her warm, soft pussy long after his hard-on subsided.

"You okay?" he whispered, suddenly petrified he'd hurt her somehow.

"Oh, yeah," she said with such satisfaction in her voice that he relaxed immediately. "You?"

"I've never been better," Willis told her. "Am I crushing you?"

"No!" she exclaimed without hesitation. "I like it. Like having you still inside me, on top of me...I feel as if nothing could ever harm me. Safe."

"You are," Willis said firmly. "But how about we do this..." He pushed a hand under her ass and held on tight as he rolled until she was draped over him. He kept his hand where it was and wiggled a bit, making sure he was still lodged inside her, then reached for a blanket with his other hand. He brought it over her back and was thrilled when she snuggled into him, resting her head on his shoulder. "How's this?"

"Perfect," she breathed.

Her warm breath wafted over his shoulder and Willis smiled at the feeling.

"Greg?"

"Yeah, little one?"

He felt her smile against him at hearing the term of endearment. He couldn't help it, compared to him, she *was* little.

"Thank you."

"For what?"

"Everything. For realizing I was struggling when I got out of that taxi. For taking care of Princess. For being there when that guy opened my door. Letting me come over here. Making me feel safe. For the orgasm...or both of them. For everything, I guess."

"You don't have to thank me for any of that. It's my pleasure...and honor."

She shook her head against him. "You're different from most men. It's almost as if you're from a different era."

"Elle always told me I should've been a Viking or something," Willis said, then stiffened. Shit, he probably shouldn't keep talking about his wife, especially when his cock was still inside her.

But Maylah nodded against him. "She was right."

"Does it bother you?" Willis blurted.

"Hearing you talk about Elle? No. She was a part of your life. An important part. Just as Ted was a part of mine. We loved them, and nothing will change that."

She was right. Willis relaxed even more.

"I'm gonna fix this for you," he said in a harder tone than he meant to use. "That guy isn't going to touch you again."

"I know," Maylah said, her voice sounding slurred.

She constantly amazed and surprised him. A lot of women would want to ask a million questions about what he might have planned. About what he was going to do. They might shy away from him using violence, if necessary, to keep her safe. But Maylah was practically asleep in his arms. The trust she was displaying seeped into his soul.

"I should move," she mumbled.

Willis' hand on her ass tightened as he pressed her into him. "Stay," he ordered.

"If I get too heavy, just shove me to the side," she told him.

Yeah, right. *That* wasn't going to happen. "Okay," he said, placating her.

One moment she was smiling against his bare shoulder, and the next she was sleeping deeply, her breaths brushing over his skin.

Willis stared up at the ceiling and let his mind drift. Most nights he had a hard time falling asleep, his brain going over cases and what he needed to do the next day. But tonight, even though he had a lot he needed to accomplish, he couldn't think about anything other than the amazing woman in his arms.

CHAPTER EIGHT

THE NEXT TWO days were both strange and mundane at the same time. When they woke up the morning after making love, Maylah was still in Greg's arms. At some point in the middle of the night she'd shifted to the side and curled up against him. His arm was around her and she was using his shoulder as a pillow.

She and Ted had shared a bed, of course they did, but they slept on their own sides, basically out of habit. She'd loved going to sleep and waking up in his arms, and things between them were as comfortable as if they'd woken up together like that every day of their lives.

He'd gotten out of bed, completely naked and relaxed in his own skin, and had taken her hand, leading her into the bathroom. They'd showered together, then he'd carefully checked out her arm and leg, putting on the antibiotic cream the doctor ordered before helping her get dressed.

They'd taken Princess out back together, and gone online and ordered groceries. Later that day, Greg had taken her back to her brownstone to pack a bag, remaining on watch the entire time.

The last two days, she'd stayed in Greg's brownstone with him. They did their own thing during the day; she played with Princess, he worked on the computer and made phone calls. But she didn't feel as if she was intruding or in the way at all. Being around Greg was wonderful. It should've been weird, since everything had happened so fast, but instead it simply felt right.

They'd cooked together, ate, watched TV, and made love. Maylah had never been happier and would've thought her life was perfect...if it wasn't for the danger she could feel hovering just out of reach.

Greg promised that she was safe, and while inside his home, she felt that way. But she couldn't hide out here forever. She refused to let her carjacker turn her into a hermit. Well, more of one than she already was.

"I need to take Princess to the rescue coordinator today. She wants to see how she's progressing," Maylah told Greg after breakfast. They'd been lazy and had hung out in bed after waking up. Well, maybe *hung out* might not be the right expression. Maylah had wanted to get her hands on Greg the night before, but he'd driven her out of her head with his mouth and tongue and any thought of reciprocating had flown from her mind.

But that morning, she'd shifted down his body while he was still asleep, and by the time he'd woken up, her mouth was already around his quickly hardening cock. He hadn't let her explore for nearly long enough before he'd turned the tables and had her straddling his face as he ate her out.

"I'm not sure that's a good idea," he said slowly.

"I can't stay here locked behind your doors forever," she protested gently.

"I know, but my informants haven't locked down Zero's location yet," he said.

Maylah knew Greg had been on the phone constantly with several confidential informants around the city he'd formed relationships with. For reasons she didn't entirely understand, they seemed loyal to Greg. They were criminals, drug dealers, and all-around immoral men, but it was more than obvious that they were intimidated by—maybe even scared of—Greg.

Which baffled Maylah, because looking at him, Greg wasn't the kind of man you'd be scared of at first glance. Then again, she'd only seen his protective side. His loving side. But after listening to his conversations with the men he'd called, who'd also been in touch with him in regard to her carjacker, she supposed she could partly understand their desire to stay on his good side. Because when Greg got riled up, his voice changed—and the thought of ever being on the receiving end of that cold and deadly tone made Maylah shiver.

"He wins if I'm too scared to leave the house," she said.

Greg closed his eyes and sighed. Then he opened them and nodded. "Okay."

"Okay? You'll take me to the organizer's house with Princess?"

"Yes. On one condition."

"What's that?"

"You stay in my sight at all times."

Maylah smiled. "What if I have to pee?" she joked. But Greg's expression didn't change. "Right, use the restroom before we leave, check," she mumbled.

Greg walked over to her and put his hands on her shoulders. "I won't lose you like I did Elle and Molly."

Maylah put her hands on his hips as she stared up at him. "This isn't the same," she protested.

"Isn't it? Zero isn't happy that you got away. That

you've been talking to the cops. He doesn't want to go back to prison, and he'll do anything to ensure that doesn't happen...including making sure the only witness can't testify against him. He's also not happy the streets are turning against him. He wanted to come to DC and be the big man on campus, so to speak. Me putting so much pressure on him is making that impossible. He's been backed into a corner, and I don't put anything past him at this point. I'm sure he's watching and waiting for the perfect chance to strike. When I'm with you, I can protect you, but if he gets an opening, he'll make a move. So I need you to stay in my sight at all times so I can prevent that from happening."

"For how long?" Maylah whispered with a small shiver. She didn't like the thought of the man who'd held her at gunpoint and threatened her with that knife getting his hands on her again. She wouldn't be as lucky the second time, she knew that without a shadow of a doubt. But she also didn't like to think about being a prisoner in her own home...or Greg's home, as nice as the last few days had been. She wasn't very social, but she preferred to shop for her own groceries instead of with a click of a mouse. She needed to get a new car, needed to feel as if she could go about her business without constantly having to look over her shoulder.

"Not much longer. My contacts are on this."

"What are they going to do?" she whispered, almost afraid to ask.

"Run him out of town."

"That's it?" Maylah asked. "Will that work? Will that make him forget about me?"

Greg sighed and pressed his lips together.

"It won't, will it?"

"I doubt it. But I only order hits if there's no other way to end someone's reign of terror."

Maylah stared at him for a long moment. "Have you done that a lot? Ordered people killed?" She hadn't missed that little tidbit when he'd told her he was "gray" earlier.

Greg's nostrils flared. "Right. It's probably good we're talking about this now. Getting it out in the open. You need to know the kind of man I am. Yeah, little one, as I've already told you, I've ordered people killed. But you have to understand, these weren't men or women who were redeemable. They had plenty of chances to turn their lives around. They didn't."

Maylah's mind spun, trying to think of what a person might have to do for Greg to order their death. "Give me an example," she said after a moment. "I need to know."

Greg's hands moved from her shoulders down to her hands. He grasped one and towed her toward the couch. He sat and pulled her down next to him, holding her hand with a grip that was a touch too tight, but Maylah didn't complain.

"There was this guy in South America. He was the head of a sex trafficking ring. He had women kidnapped from around the world, depending on what his customers desired. He held them hostage and accepted money from men who came to have sex with them against their wills. And I'm talking *years*, Maylah. Not just once or twice. Then it came to light that he was involved in trading children. When the women he kidnapped got pregnant, he allowed them to have their babies, then he groomed them to give away to perverted men. *That's* the kind of person I've ordered to be taken out."

Maylah swallowed hard and shivered. Yeah, the world was better off without someone like that in it. "Okay."

"Before you think of me as a monster, most of my energy is focused toward rescuing women and children from various situations. I hire men, and sometimes women, to rescue people who've been kidnapped. Both in the US and internationally. I have a vast network of contacts. People who are loyal to me. And yes, they're compensated for what they do. I choose former special forces men, and women, who are more than capable of doing what is asked of them."

"Wow, I had no idea," Maylah said, her respect for the man growing. She supposed she should be upset at the thought of him holding the lives of people in the palm of his hand...but she couldn't. She respected Greg even more for doing what needed to be done to keep people safe.

"And you shouldn't. People like you, sweet and innocent, shouldn't have to think about any of that. You should be able to go to the grocery store, go for a walk, get gas, without having to worry about being taken hostage and abused. If Zero doesn't get a clue, if he doesn't grow a brain, I'll end him. Without remorse. No one threatens what's mine. And make no mistake, Maylah—you're mine. Even if we go our separate ways, even if you decide you can't deal with what I do for a living, you're still under my protection. As is this neighborhood, my coworkers, the men and women I hire out. I'll do whatever it takes to keep the bubble around those I care about strong and safe. Zero made the mistake of getting inside my bubble. If he's smart, he'll back off, realize his fuck-up, and disappear. But if not..." His voice trailed off.

"You'll kill him?" Maylah mustered up the courage to ask.

"Me? No. I won't touch him. I don't have to," Greg said simply. "I have people for that."

Maylah tried to keep a straight face, but knew she'd failed when Greg asked, "What? What's funny?"

"Nothing. It's just…hearing you say, 'I have people for that.' It just struck me as funny. Like something some arrogant billionaire would say when someone asked how he made his garden look so nice."

To her relief, Greg's lips twitched. "Not quite the same, little one."

She sobered. "I know. But if you think telling me all this is going to turn me off, or make me push you away, you're wrong. I admit that I don't love knowing that danger seems to always be a step away from you, but I trust you to know what you're doing and not to end up behind bars yourself."

"Never," Greg said forcefully. "I told you before, I'm gray. I walk a fine line, but I have contacts high up in the government and in law enforcement."

"Okay."

"Okay?" he asked with a tilt of his head.

"Okay," Maylah confirmed. "You're a badass in a suit. You might look like a computer geek, but you're a scary assassin controller who doesn't tolerate evil. I can live with that."

"You can?" Greg asked, looking completely shocked.

"Yes. So I can call Roberta and tell her we'll be over later with Princess?"

Greg stared at her for so long, Maylah was beginning to get concerned. Then he shocked her by saying, "Yes...as long as it's just a check-in and not a drop-off."

"What?"

"I want to adopt her. Princess. We can go, and you can show the rescue group how well she's doing, but I don't want to leave her there. She's had enough people break her trust. I won't be another. She's just beginning to relax, and uprooting her all over again won't be good for her."

That was the moment Maylah fell in love.

She'd already been heading down that road, but hearing Greg say that he didn't want the little dog to experience any more upheaval in her life made her tumble all the way.

"Maylah? Is that okay? Do you not think I'd be an appropriate adopter? Shit, you're probably right, I'm on vacation right now, but I work too many hours, I'm gone too long, I—"

"You're perfect. Besides, I'm available to watch her during the day while you're at work. I mean, if we're still...you know."

Greg smiled then, and it was almost hard to believe he was the same man who'd just talked about ordering hits on the evilest people the world had to offer.

"Oh, we'll still be...*you know*," he told her as he stood, still holding her hand.

He then shocked the crap out of her by bending over, putting a shoulder to her belly, and heaving her up and over his shoulder.

Maylah shrieked, and Princess danced around their feet and barked as Greg headed for the stairs.

"I'm not hurting her, Princess," Greg told the dog. "Go lie down, we'll be down in a bit and we'll go for a trip...okay?"

To Maylah's surprise, Princess gave one more bark, then headed for her fluffy bed in the corner. Greg had ordered it online, and Princess had loved it at first sight.

"Where are you taking me?"

"To bed," Greg said. "To show you how sure I am that we'll be together for years and years to come."

Goose bumps broke out on Maylah's arms at his almost casual pronouncement. She smiled and stared at his ass as he carried her up the stairs like she weighed nothing. It was weird how something so good could come out of something as bad as her carjacking. But she'd learned a long time ago to live in the moment. To appreciate the here and now, because the future was always uncertain. She knew that better than most.

If Greg wanted to take her to bed in the middle of the day and show her how much he cared about her, she wasn't going to complain. Sex with this man was better than she'd ever dreamed. One day at a time. That's all she could do.

CHAPTER NINE

"YOU HAVE GOT to be shitting me," Willis said between clenched teeth. It had been three days since he'd officially adopted Princess, and almost a week since Maylah had been carjacked and he'd practically moved her into his house.

A week of bliss. Willis had never been happier, and he was so in love with the woman currently upstairs in the shower. He'd never expected to be in this situation again. He'd figured he was too old, too jaded, too much of a workaholic to ever be able to interest a woman.

Then Maylah had come crashing into his life and it was as if a light had been turned on within him. The hatred toward criminals was still there, but it was muted by Maylah's light. She was everything he wasn't, and he couldn't imagine not waking up with her plastered against his side.

She was a miracle. He'd told her what he did, and she didn't go running out the door. She actually seemed perfectly all right with it. Of course, he was currently on vacation; she might feel differently once he went back to work. But Willis had a sneaking suspicion his days of getting up at the crack of dawn and not coming home until well after dark were over.

He enjoyed what he did for a living, but Maylah was like a magnet, drawing him to her side more than the need to be at the office for hours on end.

If he could get rid of the danger that he could literally feel hovering over her, he might be able to relax completely. And if she could deal with whatever he had to do in order to keep her safe, maybe, just maybe, he'd truly believe she was really all right with who he was.

"I'm not kidding," the CI on the other end of the phone told him. "I warned him that you were losing patience and if he didn't leave town, you wouldn't be happy."

"Tell him to call me," Willis said between clenched teeth.

"You want me to give him your number? You've always told me if I gave anyone this number, you'd cut my balls off and shove them down my throat! And I believed you," the CI said in shock.

"Yeah, well, that still applies. But it's obvious this Zero asshole needs to hear straight from me that he's treading on shaky ground. Tell him to call me. Today."

"Yes, sir. Anything else?"

"You happy with this guy in your territory?" Willis asked.

"No."

The answer was short and to the point, and Willis could hear the irritation in the drug dealer's tone.

"Depending on how my talk with him goes, you have a problem getting with some of your people and taking care of business?"

"Will me or any of my friends end up in an interrogation room if we do?" the CI countered.

Willis snorted. "How long have we been working together?"

"A while."

"Right, and in that time, have I ever let you swing? Have I ever told anyone where I get my info?"

"No."

"Exactly. So no, there will be no interrogation room, as long as you're smart about things."

"Understood."

Willis nodded in satisfaction. This particular CI

was ruthless and didn't care much about anything other than money and drugs. Willis wouldn't trust him as far as he could throw him in most situations, but he'd proven to be exceptionally useful over the years by giving him information on other criminals. "I'll be in touch after I talk to Zero."

"I'll be waiting," the CI said, then ended the connection.

Greg inhaled deeply and closed his eyes.

The boards above his head, from his bedroom, creaked as Maylah walked over them, and just like that, the tension in Greg dissipated a little. The thought of her being in his house, his room...of what they'd done the night before in their bed...made him relax a fraction.

She was precisely the reason why he did what he did. Why he consorted with people like the CI. Why he dirtied his hands by ordering hits on people. He tried to counter the kill orders with even more rescue missions, but he'd always still felt dirty.

Until the last week. Just being around Maylah reminded him once more why he did what he did. It was to protect those like her. The innocents. Like Elle and Molly had been. Evil existed in the world, and if left unchecked, it would eventually take over. He refused to let that happen.

By the time she wandered down the stairs, Willis was in control of his anger. He was pissed Zero thought it was perfectly okay to take what wasn't his, and more than that, he thought it was all right to hurt a woman. Willis would never understand why some men got off on rape. Intellectually, he got that it was about power and not the sex act itself, but even that made no sense to him. It was disgusting, and as far as he was concerned, rapists should have their dicks chopped off.

"Something smells really good," Maylah said as she stood hesitantly at the edge of the kitchen.

Willis immediately held out his arm. "Come here," he ordered. He didn't like that she still seemed a little shy around him, even after how intimate they'd been.

She walked over and fitted herself against his side, and suddenly all was right in Willis' world. Having this woman at his side made him feel complete. But her hesitancy still nagged at him. "You comfortable here?" he asked.

Maylah looked up at him, her brown hair brushing her shoulders as she tipped her head back. "Yes. Why?"

"You didn't seem like you were a second ago. You want to go back to your place?"

She bit her lip then shook her head.

"Because if you do, that's okay. I get that it's hard to live out of a suitcase."

"Do you want me to go?"

"No!" Willis practically barked. He knew he'd been too harsh when Maylah flinched. He took a deep breath, trying to control the dread that filled him at the thought of Maylah leaving. Even if he knew her going back to her brownstone wouldn't mean she was leaving *him*, per se, it still felt as if he'd be losing a big chunk of himself if she went home. He turned her so she was facing him and put his hands on her face and tilted it up so he could look into her eyes as he spoke.

"You being here this last week...it's made me remember what it's like to live. Truly live. I've spent most of the last decade working myself into the ground. Partly because I was trying to outrun my grief, partly to try to get revenge against anyone who dared hurt innocent people. But mostly because I didn't want to come home to an empty house. You being here? It's a dream come true, little one. I never thought I'd ever feel like this again."

"Feel like what?" she asked quietly.

"Happy," Willis said succinctly.

"Greg," she protested with a small frown.

"I probably should've said this before now, but I don't mind you being here. And I'm not talking about what we do in the bedroom, although that's been pretty damn spectacular. It's having someone to talk to. About something other than work. I didn't realize how much planning went into the Fourth of July picnic the neighborhood throws every year. Or how fun it was to watch *Wheel of Fortune* with someone else...even though I still think you cheat because I don't know how you can guess the phrases with only a couple letters." He smiled down at her.

"I like having you here, Maylah. You make me feel...normal. And trust me, that's a damn miracle, as I know I'm anything but. With all that said, if you aren't comfortable and you want to go back to your space, I understand. It's safe; I changed all the locks, and with those security cameras I put up the other day, you'll be able to see who's at your front and back doors when they get within twenty feet. And I'm always a hop, skip, and a jump away. If you need me, all you have to do is call or text and I'm there."

"I know," she said, wrapping her arms around him.

Willis did the same, keeping her in a tight embrace. "Then what is it? What's bothering you?"

She was quiet so long, Willis wasn't sure she was going to talk to him. Then she sighed.

"I feel guilty that I'm so happy," she said softly, looking at his throat rather than in his eyes.

His heart cracked at hearing her admission. But he also understood. Probably more than she knew.

"For years, any time I so much as smiled, I felt as if I was betraying Elle and Molly," Willis told her. "What right did I have to be happy when their last moments on earth were so horrifying? Were they wondering why I hadn't found them? If I'd stopped looking? It took me years, but I finally was able to think about things in a different light. Elle was the most patient and forgiving woman I've ever met. I know without a doubt that she wouldn't want her death to make me a bitter, angry man for the rest of my life. She'd want me to live. To honor her and Molly's memory. I admit that I haven't done a great job at doing that so far, but I'm getting there."

He wanted to add that it wasn't until the last week that he thought he might just be able to do what his wife would've wanted...live a happy life...but he figured it was probably a bit too early for that admission.

"I just...when I came downstairs and saw you in the kitchen, I realized that I hadn't even thought about Ted in a few days," Maylah said softly.

Willis nodded. "You felt guilty."

"Yeah. It's not that I don't like being here, I do. I feel safe with you, and I'm happy. I just...I'm torn between being sad that Ted isn't here anymore and beyond thrilled that I'm with you."

Willis pulled her closer and hugged her hard. "I get it. I do. Things have moved really fast with us, and it's going to take some getting used to on both our parts. But please don't shut me out. I want to hear all about your good and bad times with your husband, and I'd love to have someone to share memories of my wife and daughter with. But there's no rush...even if we've fast forwarded things between us."

Maylah nodded against him. "I don't want to leave," she mumbled into his chest. "If that's okay."

"It's more than okay," Willis reassured her. "Maylah?"

She tilted her head back to look at him. "Yeah?"

"Things are going to go back to normal for you. I'm going to make sure you're not in any danger. You'll be able to do all the things you did before last week. Shop, get gas, go for walks with your fosters. Will you trust me to do that for you?"

"I trust you, Greg. I just don't want you to get in trouble in the process."

Willis' lips twitched. This woman had no idea how vast his network was. But that was all right. Their worlds were completely different; she rescued dogs and cats, nurtured them back to both physical and mental health, and he used his resources to track down and eliminate the worst of humanity.

"I won't," he promised. From here on out, he'd be even more careful than he'd been in the past. The last thing he wanted was to cause this woman one ounce of angst.

A small whine sounded at their feet, and Willis looked down to see Princess looking up at them.

"Hey, girl," he cooed. "You hungry?"

The small dog yipped as if she understood exactly what he'd asked. And she probably had. She was a smart little thing. Had probably already learned to associate the word hungry with food.

"You good?" Willis asked Maylah.

She gave him a small smile and nodded.

"Okay. How about if later we go to the store and get some more stuff for Princess?" he asked.

Maylah grinned. "You mean the pillow and the three toys we got yesterday aren't enough?"

"Nope. She needs a princess outfit, new bowls, I want to get some of those small training treats and see what we can teach her, and a couple more beds wouldn't hurt. The kitchen floor is hard and it can't be comfortable for her to sit in here while we're cooking."

Maylah burst out laughing. "Greg, she was found

sleeping in trash on the hard ground. I don't think your floor fazes her."

"All the more reason to give her everything she's never had," Willis said earnestly.

"Yeah. You're right. But...is it safe? I mean, have you heard from your people about that guy? Did Detective Greer call? Has he been caught?"

"You're safe with me," Willis said a bit too harshly. Then he took a deep breath. "I mean it, when you're with me, nothing will happen. I give you my word."

"Okay. I trust you."

Her trust in him made Willis even more determined not to let anything happen to this woman. "How're your scrapes today?" he asked in a gruff voice to try to cover up how much her words meant to him.

"They're okay. At the itchy stage," she said with a shrug.

"Which means they're healing. All right. Let me feed Princess, then I'll serve you, my queen. Have a seat," he said, pulling back and leading her to his small table.

"How about if I finish breakfast while you feed Princess?" she countered.

Willis wasn't surprised at her offer. She wasn't the kind of woman who liked to sit around and be waited on.

"Deal. The muffins should be done in a minute or two, you can take them out of the oven, and maybe scramble the eggs. They're all ready to go in the bowl by the stove, along with the chopped ham, peppers, and cheese." It had only been a week, but Willis already knew Maylah liked lots of cheese with her eggs, and enough salsa and sour cream to drown out any and all taste of the eggs themselves. He liked to add the meat and veggies to round out the breakfast a bit.

"Sounds good. Thanks, Greg."

"For what?"

"For everything."

He lifted one of her hands and kissed her fingers. "I should be thanking *you*. Without you here, my vacation would be complete and utter torture."

She laughed. "What vacation? We both know you'd have your head buried in your computer more than you already do if I wasn't here."

She wasn't wrong. But Willis realized with a jolt that with her around, he had no desire to get lost in work...for the first time in a very long time. He was content to talk with her, watch house remodeling shows, and fuss over Princess. It was amazing how much his life had changed in the last week, and he wouldn't have it any other way.

CHAPTER TEN

Maylah watched with a grin on her face as Greg methodically took each dog bed off the shelf and put it on the floor, then placed Princess on it to see if she liked it. It was cute as hell, and it made her heart melt.

"What do you think of this one, Princess?" Greg asked as he placed a therapeutic cushion on the floor. Princess sniffed it, then turned to the bright pink fuzzy faux fur one that was next to it. She climbed into the pink bed and lay down.

"Guess that settles that," Greg said with a smile.

"I'm going to go to the next aisle and look at the treats while you and Princess test out the other four thousand beds," Maylah told him.

"We should be done here in a minute or two," Greg told her.

But Maylah snorted. "That's what you said ten minutes ago. It'll be fine. I'll be right over there," she said, pointing toward her left.

Amazingly, as reticent as she'd been that morning to leave the house, she was feeling very good about the outing right now. They'd stopped at the grocery store before coming to the pet supply shop, and having Greg at her side made her confidence grow. Watching how observant he was, how he constantly scanned their surroundings for threats, allowed her to relax.

"All right. We'll come find you in a few minutes. Get the really small treats, if they have any. We don't want Princess getting fat," Greg warned.

Maylah laughed. "Right." There was no chance in hell that the dog wouldn't put on weight. Greg was constantly worried about her eating, and she'd seen him sneak her human food on more than one occasion. That dog already had him wrapped around her little paw...and Maylah couldn't have been happier. Princess deserved to be spoiled after everything she'd been though.

Maylah stopped in the middle of the treat aisle at that thought. If Princess deserved to be spoiled...why didn't *she*? If all the dogs and cats she'd fostered deserved a better life, a happy one, why couldn't she let herself feel the same?

It clicked then. Ted dying had been awful. Finding his body had been horrifying. But his death didn't mean she never deserved to be happy again. And she was. Happy. Because of Greg. He was easy to be around. Made her feel completely comfortable in his presence. She felt as if she could be exactly who she was...not have to put on a fake persona to impress him.

And while the time was coming when she probably needed to go back to her home, she was enjoying spending so much time with Greg. She hadn't missed how stressed he'd sounded when he'd asked if she wanted to go home. The truth was...Greg's brownstone felt more like home than her own place ever had. She'd moved there after Ted had died to get a fresh start, and even though she loved the building and the neighborhood, a part of her had always felt disconnected from the space.

But from the first moment Greg had carried her into his townhouse, she'd felt as if she'd come home.

Maylah smiled at the thought. She supposed she should be freaking out that she'd basically moved in with Greg after a day, and without a second thought, but since he seemed just as happy to have her there as she was to be there, she couldn't be too worried about it.

She'd been so lost in her thoughts that she'd

missed the man walking down the aisle toward her until he was almost on top of her. She heard footsteps, looked up, and froze.

This wasn't the man who'd carjacked her, but he still scared the crap out of her.

He was tall, probably around six-two, and very muscular. He had on a baggy pair of black cargo pants and a white tank top. He had tattoos all over his arms and up his neck. He even had a couple of black crosses tattooed on his cheeks. And his intense focus was squarely on *her*.

She made a small sound in the back of her throat, but was too scared to make any kind of noise.

"Maylah Brant?" the man asked in a low, rumbly tone.

She took a single step backward, trying to force her legs to move more, but she couldn't. Every muscle in her body was frozen.

Then she heard a deep growl from behind her, and Princess was there, between her and the scary-looking man, growling menacingly as if she was ten times the size she was.

"Step back, Boo," Greg ordered from behind her.

Then his arm was around her waist and he pulled her backward, so he was standing between her and the stranger.

"Willis," the man said with a nod.

"What the fuck? You're scaring her."

"Sorry. I didn't mean to. I brought these," the tattooed man said, holding something out to Greg.

"I don't care what you brought. You know my rules," Greg said, sounding as if he was two seconds from losing it.

"I know, never approach you in public. But one of my guys got these off Zero, and I thought you'd want them back. Thought your lady would want them."

Peering around Greg, Maylah saw what the man was holding. "My keys!" she exclaimed softly.

Greg reached out and snatched the keys from his palm. "Fine. You did what you set out to. Now get gone."

"Also wanted to see your lady in person. Need to be able to describe her to my network. Help spread the word that she's off limits."

The man Greg had called "Boo" winked at Maylah, and she was surprised to find herself relaxing. He looked scary, yes, but now that she could think straight, she didn't get any serial killer vibes from him. He obviously wasn't a man to cross, but at the moment, she didn't feel as if she was in danger.

He turned his attention to Greg, and Maylah saw a change come over him. His voice got harder and his eyes narrowed. "Head's up, Zero's not happy. He's not finding any customers and he's getting desperate to offload the shit he bought. He blames you and your lady."

"You give him my number?" Greg asked.

Boo nodded.

"I'll make it clear it's in his best interest to move on when he calls," Greg told him.

"Watch your back," Boo said. "I'll do what I can to spread the word about your lady, but this Zero guy is unhinged. He's paranoid, and he clearly thinks all his problems will end if he finishes what he started."

Greg nodded, and Maylah took a step closer to him. Every muscle in his body was rock hard. She put a hand on his back and felt him flinch before he pushed back into her touch a fraction.

"Princess, sit," Greg said sternly.

To Maylah's surprise, Princess sat back on her haunches. She hadn't stopped growling at Boo, but at least it didn't look as if she was about to eat him anymore.

"Nice dog," Boo said almost conversationally.

"Thank you for the keys. How's the wife and kids?"

Boo grinned, and it almost made him look boyish. "They're good. Spoiled as hell, but I wouldn't have it any other way."

Greg nodded.

"Anyway, I'll await your call as to what happens

next. Ma'am," he said, nodding at Maylah. "I apologize if I scared you. I'm harmless."

Greg snorted in response.

To her surprise, Maylah found herself saying, "Be careful out there. I have it on good authority that it can be dangerous."

Boo chuckled. "Right." Then he turned to Greg. "I understand completely why you're so determined to shut down this Zero guy. Sweet pussy like that needs to be protected. Later."

Maylah would've normally been offended by being referred to as "sweet pussy," but for some reason, she couldn't find it in her to care. Boo wasn't a man she would ever consider being friends with, but it was clear while he was into some nefarious dealings, he wasn't evil.

"Shit, I'm so sorry," Greg said as he turned to her.

But Maylah shook her head. "It's okay."

"No, it's not," Greg insisted. "My contacts know the rules. They're not supposed to be seen with me—or within five miles of me. He screwed up by coming here today."

"How'd he even know we'd be here?"

Greg shrugged. "There are no secrets on the streets. Word travels faster than you'd ever believe. It's why my CIs are so vital to what I do. They hear shit way before the cops can sniff it out."

Maylah was beginning to understand that.

"I'll deal with him later," Greg said.

"I do appreciate having my keys back. But keys are no good without my car," she said tentatively.

"I'm sure your car is safe. He wouldn't have even bothered bringing your keys if it wasn't. Hell, it's probably parked outside your brownstone."

"Really?" Maylah asked, her brows shooting upward.

"Yup."

"Huh. That's...okay, that's kind of awesome."

For the first time, the stress lines around Greg's eyes and mouth smoothed out as he shook his head in exasperation.

"What's his story? I mean, he looks completely scary, but he seemed kind of...soft?"

Greg snorted again. "He's not soft. Not in the least."

"Okay, but...don't get mad, but he reminds me a little of you. Super protective."

Greg shrugged. "He is. He loves his old lady. He's got eight kids. All girls. He's a drug dealer, would slit the throat of anyone who steals from him or crosses him. But with his family, he's a different man. He doesn't tolerate anyone who reneges on money they owe him, or who tries to take over his territory, and he doesn't condone violence against women or kids."

"So he's gray...like you said you were," Maylah said.

Greg stared at her for a long moment.

"What?" she asked when he didn't comment.

"I just...you look so damn innocent on the outside. But you get it. Get *me*."

Maylah stepped into his personal space and put her hand on his cheek. "I get you," she agreed.

Greg's head came down and he kissed her right there in the middle of the dog treat aisle. He wrapped an arm around her and pressed against the small of her back, plastering her body against his own. The kiss wasn't gentle, it was one of the kisses he usually gave her right before he sank deep into her body.

When he pulled back, they were both breathing hard. Maylah could feel his hard cock against her belly. "I want you," she whispered.

He grinned. "I think it's obvious how I feel."

Princess whined at their feet. Greg looked down and took a deep breath. He leaned down and picked up the little dog and cuddled her between them. "Who's a good girl?" he asked in a high-pitched baby-talk tone.

Maylah snickered.

"Don't laugh. She was the one who realized something was wrong. She bolted off the bed and around to this aisle," Greg told her.

Maylah put her hand on Princess' head and stroked her gently. "Good girl," she praised.

Greg looked at her with a serious expression on his face. "Boo was right."

"Boo," Maylah said with a small shake of her head. "I can't believe that's his name."

Greg smiled, then got serious again. "Street name. His real name is Theodore. But don't ever call him that."

Maylah pantomimed zipping her lips shut.

"Anyway, he was right. It's good that he saw you in person. He can describe you to his network. The more people who know who you are to me, and what you look like, the better."

"What am I to you?" Maylah asked, then immediately regretted it.

But Greg didn't even hesitate. "You're mine."

He'd said that before. And Maylah supposed many women would resent it. Wouldn't want to be referred to by such a possessive term. But since she *wanted* to be Greg's, she wasn't offended in the least.

Greg might have called her his, but he was hers right back.

"You like that," he said, studying her intently.

Maylah shrugged. "Yeah," she said simply.

"Damn. Now I really need to be inside you," he grumbled.

"How about we grab some treats, get whatever bed you and Princess have decided is the best, and get home?"

Without a word, Greg pocketed the keys he still had in his fist, shifted Princess in his grasp, and took Maylah by the hand. She had time to grab a couple bags of treats before he towed her back to the other aisle. The pink fluffy bed was still on the floor and without a word, Maylah leaned over to grab it. It was obvious Greg wasn't going to let go of her hand, and his other one was full with Princess.

Greg's head was on a swivel as they checked out, making sure there wouldn't be any other surprises. They drove home without much conversation and Maylah was delighted to see her simple Toyota Camry parked in front of her brownstone, just as Greg said it would be. She wasn't ready to leap in and head out on her own again, there were too many bad memories associated with the car that she needed to work through, but she was still glad it was returned.

"I'll call the detective later about the car," Greg murmured as he parked. "Stay there," he ordered as he opened his door. He came around to her side and helped her out, then tucked her hand in the crook of his arm as he ordered Princess to "do her business."

Then the three of them walked into his brownstone together. He left Maylah to put Princess' bed in the kitchen and to put the treats away as he went back outside to grab the groceries they'd bought before going to the pet supply store.

They worked together to put everything perishable in the fridge, but as soon as that was done, he petted Princess, told her she was a good girl, then towed Maylah toward the stairs.

She giggled as she tripped along behind him. "In a hurry?" she asked.

"Yup," he said with a nod and without slowing down.

Maylah didn't complain, because she wanted the same thing Greg did.

CHAPTER ELEVEN

IT WAS two days before Zero finally called. Willis wasn't surprised. The guy obviously thought he was in control, calling on his timetable rather than Willis'.

Maylah was in the backyard with Princess, trying to teach her to play fetch. The little dog wasn't having any of it though. She'd run after the ball or stick that Maylah threw, but then decided that playing keep away was much more fun than simply doing Maylah's bidding.

Willis was smiling as he watched them in the backyard, loving how relaxed Maylah seemed. Seeing Boo had rattled her, but she'd rallied quickly. It had taken a little coercion, but Willis had finally gotten her to admit that she was uncomfortable with the thought of getting back into her car, and he'd already made mental plans to replace it. He didn't blame her.

After being carjacked and having to jump out of the moving vehicle, he wouldn't be all fired up to get back inside either.

Little by little, she was returning to normal...or what he figured was her normal, at least. She smiled often and seemed more relaxed. She didn't seem eager to go back to her own place, which didn't upset Willis in the least. If he had his way, she'd never go back.

The thought should've had him freaking out, but instead if felt...right. He'd always been a man who knew what he wanted, and he wanted Maylah Brant. Wanted her in his bed, his home, his life.

But first, he needed to neutralize the threat against her. And Zero was a threat. He knew that to his bones. He'd dealt with his share of evil, and after all the research he'd done on Zero, he understood that was exactly what the man was.

Not too smart, though. He'd been telling anyone who would listen that he was going to eliminate the only person who could identify him. It was apparently his MO. He bragged about killing over a dozen "bitches" after kidnapping and raping them. Claimed the cops hadn't been able to make any charges stick because there were no witnesses alive to finger him.

That wasn't going to happen to Maylah, no way in hell. Zero was a dead man walking. Willis had been content to warn the man and let him leave the DC area, but after learning of his penchant for raping and killing women, that option was no longer on the table.

Willis had planned on using Boo and his network to eliminate Zero, but after some consideration, he decided he needed some outside assistance. The men of Silverstone had been four of his best assassins, but now that they had families of their own, they'd asked to be taken off the list of Willis' operatives—except for special circumstances.

He figured one or two of them wouldn't object to taking care of this job for him. Especially when they heard about Maylah.

Looking down at his phone when it rang, Willis saw the number was unknown. The hair on the back of his neck stood up. He instinctively knew this was Zero finally calling. It could've been a telemarketer, but it wasn't. Willis knew it down to his toes.

"Willis," he barked as a greeting.

"Oh, so official," Zero taunted. "You shouldn't have given me your number. Do you know the chaos I can cause for you as a result?" He laughed, and it was a malevolent sound.

"I'm glad you called. I was going to give you a chance. Tell you to get out of town. But I've changed my mind," Willis told him as he watched Maylah laugh at Princess' antics.

"Fuck you," Zero growled. "I don't give a shit what you think or what you want. You can't make me do nothin'. I'm gonna find that bitch and finish what I started. I'll fuck her so hard she's bleeding from every orifice, then I'll use my knife to fuck her as well, carving her up from the inside out. She'll be *begging* to die by the time I'm done with her."

Willis refused to let his words get to him. He concentrated on the faint sound of Maylah's laughter from outside. She tried to grab the little dog, but Princess darted to the right just in time, making Maylah fall to the ground instead.

"You're a dead man," Willis told him matter-of-factly.

Zero laughed. "And you're delusional. You can't catch me. No one can."

"You keep on thinking that," Willis said. "It won't be me, but you'll know before the bullet enters your brain that I sent your executioners."

"You're full of shit, old man. I've seen you. You have a huge stick up your ass, you're skinnier than Pee Wee Herman, and pasty white from sitting behind a computer all day. I'm not scared of you. You should be more worried about *me*. Of what I'm going to do to that fat bitch you've got locked inside your house, thinking she's safe. Maybe I'll take that damn dog too, return its head to you in a box."

"You won't be the first person to underestimate me, and you won't be the last," Willis said calmly.

But Zero's next words smashed his calm to pieces.

"The bitch looks real nice today in her white shirt and those ugly-as-shit pink shorts. Her blood will look amazing against that shirt."

Willis stiffened as he stared out the window. Maylah wore one of his FBI T-shirts and a pair of sleep shorts she hadn't bothered to change out of yet. He thought she looked adorable. And he hated knowing that Zero was seeing what should've been for his eyes only.

Doing everything possible to stay calm, Willis walked to the back door and opened it, gesturing for Maylah to come back inside.

She immediately headed his way, Princess at her heels, instinctually realizing playtime was over.

Zero chuckled. "Smart man. But you can't protect her. Not from me. I'm gonna get her. Maybe not today, maybe not tomorrow, but someday soon. And you'll have to live with knowing that you couldn't protect her."

No. He wouldn't. Not ever again. Willis had enough guilt about his wife and daughter on his soul, he wouldn't add Maylah to his life's regrets as well.

Maylah came to his side and looked up at him in concern as he closed and locked the back door behind her. Ever aware that she was listening, he said, "You've hurt your last woman, Zero," he said in a low, deadly tone.

The guy laughed again. "Whatever, old man. I'm just getting started. You better fuck the bitch nice and hard tonight, because soon she'll be stone-cold dead—and the last cock she'll know is mine."

The line went dead, and it took Willis a moment to move.

"Greg?" Maylah whispered. "Are you okay?"

"I will be," he said slowly, then hugged her tight. She was fine. Warm and alive. And he'd do whatever it took to keep her that way. He wasn't about to scare her further by telling her Zero had been watching her and Princess. He wanted to rush out of the house and search for the asshole himself, but that would leave Maylah alone and vulnerable...and was probably exactly what Zero was hoping he'd do.

He'd have to leave Zero to others. In the past, he might've been bitter about that, resented the fact that he couldn't be involved in taking him down. But over the years he'd learned patience, and he understood that eliminating evil was just as satisfying no matter who wielded the sword, so to speak.

"You want to watch another episode of *Game of*

Thrones?" he asked, forcing himself to sound as normal as possible.

"I want to do whatever it'll take to make you relax. To wipe that awful look of anger and frustration off your face," Maylah countered.

Willis looked down at her and forced his muscles to loosen. "Popcorn, peanut butter M&Ms, Dr Peppers, and you snuggled up against my side in our bed. That'll do it."

She gave him a small smile. "Then that's what you'll get."

"If you pop the popcorn and gather the other stuff, I'll be up in a few. I have one more call I need to make," he told her.

Maylah studied him for a long moment. "Are you sure you want to watch TV? I mean, maybe you should go to the gym and pound the punching bag for an hour or so."

Willis' lips twitched upward. How this woman could coax him out of the horrible black hole he'd fallen into was beyond him. "I'll be okay. Just a short call and I'll be up."

"All right."

"And if you're naked while we're eating junk and watching dragons take over the world, all the better."

Maylah rolled her eyes. "Spoken like a true guy."

"That's because I am one."

"Yes, you are. *My* guy. Okay, Greg. Make your call, but don't take too long because my naked self will be cold up there all alone."

Amazingly, Willis felt his cock twitch in his pants. He hadn't been this horny in years. Shouldn't be this ready to go at his age. But this woman simply did it for him. "Five minutes," he told her.

"I'll be waiting," she said with a smile. She went up on her tiptoes, kissed his lips in a short, hard kiss, then headed for the kitchen, Princess at her heels.

Taking a deep breath, Willis dialed a number he hadn't called in at least a year. When the man on the other end answered, Willis said, "Hey, Bull. It's Willis. I need a favor."

To his relief, Bull immediately said, "Name it."

It took a little more than five minutes to bring his old contact up to speed about what was happening, about Maylah and how Willis was going to marry her as soon as he could possibly arrange it, and giving him Boo's contact info so he could get location details on Zero. But by the time he hung up, Willis was confident that the threat to his woman would be over and done with before the end of the week.

Feeling better than he had since before seeing Maylah climbing out of the taxi hurt and limping, Willis headed for the stairs.

CHAPTER TWELVE

"I DON'T KNOW ABOUT THIS," Maylah said as she nibbled on her thumbnail and she stared at the fully loaded XC90 Volvo SUV. She loved it, of course she did, but it was way more expensive than her Camry, and she wasn't sure she was comfortable with Greg helping with the payments.

"I am," Greg said firmly. "It's top of the line, the safety features are unbeatable, and you'll be safe in it. Look at me, little one."

Maylah lifted her gaze to his.

"Tell me honestly, would you be able to get into your Camry right this moment without having any kind of flashback?"

She wanted to lie, but couldn't. She shook her head.

"Right. Why do that to yourself? You said you

293

could afford to upgrade your car, so this is a good time to do it. We're getting a great price, and this is a very reliable vehicle."

They *were* getting a good deal on the car. Maylah was sure that was because of Greg and his connections. But it felt somewhat wasteful, considering her Camry was still running perfectly fine.

"How about this? We'll take it for a test drive and see what you think," Greg said. "We were going to go and see the new foster the rescue group has, so we'll just take the Volvo out there instead of my Explorer."

"Can we do that?" Maylah asked. "The rescue is way out of the city."

Greg smiled. "It won't be a problem."

Maylah shook her head. Of course it wasn't. She turned to look at the metallic blue Volvo once more. She really did love it. And the bells and whistles were amazing. "Okay," she said softly.

She laughed when Greg yanked on her hand and she tumbled into him. But he didn't let her fall, of course. He hugged her hard, then said he'd be right back and strode toward the building, most likely to finalize the details of them taking the SUV for a few hours. She ran a hand over the side of the car...and for the first time in what seemed like forever, thought about Ted.

He'd hated buying cars. Not that she could

blame him, she wasn't a huge fan herself. But he'd drive a vehicle into the ground rather than deal with a car dealership and the salespeople. But Greg seemed right at home, and his patience was legendary.

When the first salesman who approached insisted on ignoring her and talking to Greg instead, he shut him down quickly and asked to speak to someone else. The man looked taken aback, but did as Greg requested.

Before the second salesman even opened his mouth, Greg told him, "I'm not buying a car, Maylah is. So if you insist on ignoring her and only making eye contact with me, we'll leave so fast it'll make your head spin."

The second salesman wasn't an idiot, and he'd given all his attention to Maylah.

She turned and met Greg's gaze through the windows. Even though he wasn't right by her side, he was still watching out for her. It felt really good.

His vacation was almost over, and the last two and a half weeks had been unreal. Maylah had found herself in an intense relationship and in love. It had happened so quickly, but felt so right.

Greg was on edge a little more as each day passed because the date for him to return to work was approaching...and his contacts hadn't been able to find Zero. Apparently, her carjacker was more slippery and smarter than everyone had thought.

One night, after Greg had spoken to Bull, the man he'd asked to come to DC to take care of things for him, Greg had been in an especially stressed-out mood. Maylah had finally gotten him to open up a little, and he'd said that it was too bad Zero was a psychopath, because Greg could've used him as a CI and expanded his network of people who sniffed out information when needed.

Earlier this morning, he'd apparently had enough of hiding her in his house, because he'd informed Maylah that they were going car shopping. She'd tried to protest, but finally admitted that yes, she had the money to buy a new car, and no, she wasn't overly attached to the Camry because of Ted, and yes, an SUV would be safer when she had to drive around DC traffic, especially in the winter.

She'd been surprised to see Greg come downstairs in a suit, his pants freshly pressed. She hadn't seen him in what she mentally called his "work clothes" since the night he'd helped her out of the taxi.

When she'd asked if he'd gotten called into work, he'd smiled sheepishly and said no, that he wanted to make a good impression on their possible new foster.

It was ridiculous, as the dog or cat certainly wouldn't care what they were wearing, but Maylah thought it was also the sweetest thing she'd ever heard in her life. Greg had more depth to him than she'd ever expected, and she felt like the luckiest woman in the world to have him at her side.

She was still smiling when he walked back toward her.

"Ready to go?" he asked as he approached.

"They said it was okay?"

"Yup." Greg held out the keys to her.

"You want me to drive?" she asked, somewhat surprised.

"Of course. You're the one buying the car, and you're the one who'll be driving it most of the time," Greg said.

"Wow. A lot of guys don't like to be in the passenger seat. They have some sort of internal macho thing that makes them think they have to drive. Something about being in charge."

"I'm not most guys," Greg said with a small shrug. "And for the record...you like when I take charge...at least in our bed."

Maylah could feel herself blushing. He wasn't wrong. "Whatever," she said, grabbing the keys from his hand.

Greg chuckled but didn't comment further, he simply gestured for her to climb into the driver's seat.

When she did, he closed the door, then walked around to the passenger side.

It took her a few minutes to adjust the seats comfortably and to familiarize herself with all the knobs and switches. Then she turned to Greg and asked, "You ready?"

"Ready," he said with a nod.

Surprisingly, it really did look as if he was completely comfortable with her driving. It made Maylah feel more confident about taking the expensive car out when she didn't own it yet. She pulled out onto the busy road and concentrated on where they were going.

Soon they were headed out of the city toward Roberta's house. She had a few acres of land where she could house the dogs and cats, and the occasional goat or other farm animal, that her rescue took in.

"How did you get started fostering?" Greg asked.

"I needed something to do after Ted died," Maylah said. "I was lonely, and taking care of the animals helped with my grief. Gave me something to concentrate on other than all the what-ifs that wouldn't stop spinning in my head."

Greg nodded. "I understand that. Doesn't it hurt when they get adopted though?"

Maylah smiled over at him. "A little. But the rescue group does their homework, they'd never let one of their precious charges go to anyone who might abuse them."

"I can't imagine giving Princess up," Greg admitted with a smile.

"It's just part of the process," Maylah insisted. "I can't keep all the animals I take in. If I did, I wouldn't be able to help any others. And yeah, it took *you* like three seconds to become a foster-failure." She grinned at him.

Greg didn't seem fazed. "There was something about Princess that called to me."

Maylah reached over and patted his leg. "I think it's sweet."

"That's me...Mr. Sweet," Greg said with a roll of his eyes, but he didn't hesitate to take her hand in his and bring it up to his lips. "How's the car feel?"

"Good. I thought it would seem like I was driving a huge truck after my Camry, but it's honestly not too bad. And the mirrors are big enough that I can see everything around me really easily. There aren't any blind spots. And," she grinned over at him, "I like that my speed is projected on the windshield. It's so bougie."

He laughed. "Wait until you try the massaging seat."

"Is this a car or a bed?" she asked with a smile.

They'd just turned onto the road that would ultimately lead to their destination when Maylah looked in the rearview mirror. "Um, Greg...is that car behind us too close or—"

She didn't get a chance to finish her question when a loud popping sound rang out and the car swerved almost uncontrollably.

Maylah let out a little scream and struggled to control the SUV. Another gunshot came from the car behind them and it was all she could do to keep the vehicle on the road.

"Fuck!" Greg swore as he reached over and grabbed the wheel to help her keep the car on the dirt road. There were trees on either side, but not enough to run into and hide. The countryside was a mix of flat farmlands and pockets of trees.

"Listen to me," Greg said in a tone she'd only heard from him when he was speaking on the phone with one of his mysterious CIs. "We can't outrun him, so I'm going to have to take care of this once and for all. I'm not going to let him hurt you. Do you trust me?"

Maylah felt as if she was going to hyperventilate. There was no doubt who was behind them shooting. Her fingers were white as she gripped the steering wheel. But trusting Greg? There was no question about that. "Yes."

"You didn't even hesitate," he said in an awed tone.

Maylah glanced over at him. "That's because there's no doubt in my mind that you'll keep me safe."

"Damn straight. Go ahead and stop."

Maylah looked in the rearview mirror. The red car behind them was close enough that she could easily see the man behind the steering wheel. He was smirking, and it was absolutely the same guy who'd carjacked her. She could see the pockmarks on his face, the crooked nose, the same haircut...and of course the absolute blankness in his eyes. She was scared to death and the last thing she wanted to do was stop. Zero obviously had a gun, and she didn't think Greg was carrying.

Even though it went against everything she was feeling, Maylah took her foot off the gas and brought the SUV to a stop. The dirt wafted around the SUV from the road, giving the eerie illusion that they were alone. But it would only be a matter of seconds before Zero was in their face with that damn gun.

"When I tell you to do something, I need you to do it without hesitation," Greg told her, putting a hand on her cheek. "Can you do that? I promise to get us both out of this unscathed."

Maylah nodded, although she had no idea what he

had planned. It wasn't as if he was Superman and could deflect bullets or anything.

"Good. Come on, we're getting out on my side."

It was awkward to climb over the console, but when Maylah saw Zero strolling toward her door as if he had all the time in the world, she quickly slipped out from behind the wheel and over to the passenger side.

"Looks like you have a tire problem," Zero sneered as he quickly walked around the front of the car to confront them. "I figured I'd be a good neighbor and stop to help."

"You're elusive, I'll give you that," Greg said in an almost friendly sounding tone.

Zero's eyes narrowed. "*No one* tells me where I can go and what I can do. Not even you, Mr. FBI Agent. You think your shit don't stink, but you're just like me, old man."

"Wrong," Greg countered. "I'm *nothing* like you. You're a psychopath who gets off on hurting those he thinks are weaker than him."

"*Everyone's* weaker than me," Zero said. "And those local pussies you've sent after me are amateurs. You don't own this city, and they don't own the territories they claim either."

Maylah let herself be moved backward when Greg subtly stepped in front of her.

"Come here," Zero told Maylah.

"Not happening," Greg told him.

To her surprise, Zero smiled. "She must have a magic pussy for you to be so protective of her. I was going to kill you fast," he said, tucking the gun he'd been holding in the back of his pants. "But instead, I'm going to slit your throat and let you watch as I rape her with my cock, then with the same knife I used to kill you with."

"Again—not happening," Greg said in a calm voice.

Maylah couldn't control the shaking of her entire body. She was terrified, but refused to do anything that might distract Greg. She could run off into the trees, see if she could get help, but she'd said that she trusted Greg, and she did. If he'd wanted her to run, he would've told her to do so. So she stayed where she was, petrified about what was going to happen next.

"You don't have any say. It's happening," Zero said.

It seemed they were at an impasse.

"Maylah?" Greg said almost conversationally.

"Yeah?" she whispered back.

"Close your eyes. No matter what you hear, don't open them until I tell you it's okay."

Without thought, her eyes slid shut. It was disorienting to suddenly be in the dark, but if that's what Greg wanted her to do, she would comply. She'd said she trusted him, and she did. One hundred percent.

———

Willis had never been as focused as he was right this second. He knew what he had to do, but didn't want Maylah to see it. He hated that she was scared—and he had no doubt she was petrified. He felt her entire body vibrating behind him, shaking from fear. But he'd never been as proud of someone as he was right that moment. She was holding it together. He couldn't take his eyes off the man holding the knife to check on her, to reassure her, which sucked. But Zero's cockiness would be his downfall. The man thought he'd have no problem subduing Willis—so much so that he'd actually put down his gun.

"Close your eyes. No matter what you hear, don't open them until I tell you it's okay," Willis told Maylah, praying she'd do as he asked. The last thing he wanted was for her to see what he was about to do.

He gave her three seconds to do as he asked, then he moved—pouncing on Zero in one quick lunge.

It was clear his attack surprised the other man, who reacted a fraction of a second too late.

Willis wrapped his fingers around the wrist that held the knife and he brought his knee up hard and fast right into Zero's groin. He doubled over, allowing Willis to swiftly move behind him. He forced the man upright and brought the hand holding the knife to his neck.

Zero struggled, but Willis had the strength of ten men at that moment. He spared a single second to glance at Maylah, and saw she'd crouched down next to the SUV to make herself as small as she could, and her eyes were scrunched closed.

Gratitude filled Willis—and regret. He didn't like taking lives, even though he had no problem doing what needed to be done.

Not wanting to draw this out, needing no big speeches or tough words, Willis ran the knife, which Zero still held in a death grip, across his enemy's throat before shoving the man and letting him drop to the dirt.

Zero coughed once, then gasped and twitched as the blood from his jugular, which had been neatly sliced clean through, began to pool around him on the dusty ground.

The entire attack took less than ten seconds, and for a moment, Willis regretted killing the man so fast after he'd caused such pain and hurt in the world. Then he heard a small whimper come from the side of the SUV, and all thoughts of the dead man at his feet faded.

He quickly moved to Maylah's side. He crouched next to her making sure to block any sight of Zero dying behind him. He held out a hand, reaching for her, but then saw Zero's blood on his skin. He scowled.

"Little one, it's me. You're okay. He's gone."

"Can I open my eyes?"

"Yes, but don't look anywhere but at me. Understand?"

She nodded, then opened her eyes. She lifted her head and met his gaze. "Are you okay?"

"Yes."

"Did he run?"

"No."

Maylah frowned in confusion.

"I killed him," Willis said baldly.

He wasn't sure what he expected Maylah to do or say, but she blew him away when she simply nodded. Then her gaze landed on his hand. "You're bleeding!" she exclaimed.

"It's not mine," Willis told her.

"Oh. Well...we should clean that up," she said shakily. "I've got a water bottle in the car." She stood and opened the passenger door, reached over to the center console, and grabbed the plastic bottle in the drink holder, then turned back to him. "Hold out your hand," she ordered.

Bemused, Willis did as she ordered, knowing keeping busy was likely helping her control her emotions. When she'd finished rinsing his hand off, she grabbed the sweater she'd brought with her in case she got cold and used it to dry him. "There," she said with a small nod.

"I need to make a call," Willis told her. He wanted nothing more than to take her in his arms and hold her tight. But it was only a matter of time before someone drove down this road, and he needed to get rid of Zero's body before that happened.

Maylah didn't ask who he was calling, she simply nodded.

Willis wasn't sure if she was in shock, or simply biding time before she told him that she couldn't be with someone like him...and he was too chicken to figure out if it was the former or latter at the moment.

He grabbed his phone from his pocket and dialed a number. When Bull answered, Greg said, "He found us. I took care of it. But I need you to take out the trash."

"Shit," Bull said. "I'm sorry I didn't find him before he made his move. I was close several times, but he managed to slink away like the slime he was."

"It's okay. But I need you to be quick. Maylah's here."

"She saw you take him out?"

"No, but she heard. I need to take her home."

"Give me your coordinates. I'll be there as fast as I can."

Willis gave Bull directions on how to find them. A part of him was glad his former mercenary didn't have to complete this assignment. The man had a wife—who was a kindergarten teacher, of all things—and a family. Willis wouldn't have called him in the first place if he didn't need someone he trusted with Maylah's life.

Willis pulled Maylah to the back of the SUV, away from Zero's body so she wouldn't accidentally see it, then took a deep breath as he stared at the flat tires.

Once again, the thought crept in that Zero would've been an asset if he hadn't been so damn evil. He was a good shot, a master at evasion, and was obviously smarter than anyone realized.

"Do you think there are spares inside?" Maylah asked quietly.

Willis looked at her then. *Really* looked. Her hair was disheveled, she was pale, her hands were shaking a little, but her chin was up, and he could see admiration in her eyes. For him. He was almost overcome with emotion. Looking at his hands, making sure there was no more blood on them, he reached for her.

He palmed her face and rested his forehead on hers. He felt her hands slip under his suit jacket and clench his sides. "Fuck," he whispered.

"It's okay. We're all right," she assured him.

Reality set in for Willis then. What could've happened. What he'd done. He felt weak, and his legs shook as he closed his eyes. He couldn't look at Maylah. How could she want to be with him after what he'd just done? He'd killed a man without a second thought. It had taken seconds.

"Greg? You're okay. He didn't hurt us. You prevented anything from happening."

Willis opened his eyes and lifted his head, staring down at the woman he loved more than his own life. He'd loved Elle. And his daughter. What he felt for Maylah seemed...bigger. Maybe it was because of what almost happened, maybe it was because he was older and more knowledgeable of the evils in the world—and aware he was given another chance at a love that he never thought he'd find again. Whatever the reason, he couldn't bear to lose her. Wouldn't survive if she walked away.

"I'm sorry," he choked out.

"For what?" she asked with a tilt of her head.

Willis almost laughed. Was she really asking that?

"I just killed a man. Right in front of you. And I'd do it again without a second thought." Why was he pushing the issue? Was he *trying* to push her away?

No, he was just trying to understand where her head was at. Was she in shock? Did she not comprehend what had just happened?

"A man who was hell-bent on killing you and raping me horrifically. You did what you had to do. He had a gun. And a knife. You *protected* me, Greg. And all the future women who would've suffered through what he planned on doing to me. I'm not sorry. Not in the least."

He stared at her for a beat. "You trusted me so easily," he blurted.

Maylah looked confused again. "Yeah. I did. And do."

That was it. Willis was going to marry this woman. He was going to spend the rest of his life making sure she was happy and nothing ever scared her again. He opened his mouth to say something, he had no idea what, but she beat him to it.

"It was self-defense. He's got that gun on him, and it'll have his fingerprints on it. We have the police reports about the carjacking and the threats he made, not to mention that he came to my house with the intention of hurting me. And I'm sure you can get your contacts to testify about how he wanted to kill me. I've got money saved up to bond you out if needed. We're going to get through this. I promise."

Willis blinked. "What...how..." he stammered.

Maylah gave him a small smile. "I watch a lot of crime TV."

This woman. She slayed him. "I appreciate your support, but this isn't going to go to trial. I'm not going to be arrested."

"Oh. Because of your connections?"

"Not in the way you're thinking. Because Bull is on his way—and he's going to make sure Zero disappears."

Her mouth fell open in shock, then she recovered. "Right. One of your super-secret contacts. Am I going to get to meet him?"

"Yes. He should be here soon."

"Okay. Um...will anyone miss Zero? I mean, he has to have family."

It was so like Maylah to worry about the asshole's loved ones. "He burned those bridges long ago...after he raped his own sister when she was just twelve, and again when he kidnapped and raped his sister-in-law."

"Holy crap, what a jerk!"

Amazingly, Willis felt a smile form on his lips. Only this woman could do that for him. His legs felt stronger and he took a deep breath. "As soon as Bull removes the trash, I'll call a contact of mine to come fix the tires, and we can go home."

Maylah stared at him for a long moment, her gaze going from his toes to his head, then back down.

"What are you thinking about so hard?" he asked. "Do I have any more blood on me?"

She shook her head. "Surprisingly, no. I don't know how you managed that, and I'm even more impressed and in awe of you than before. But what I was going to say was that, we're here...well, *almost* here. We might as well go and see the dog we were coming to see."

Willis blinked. "Are you sure?"

"Yes. You got all dressed up, and that dog needs us. Heck, we probably need something to take our minds off what happened, so yes, I'm sure."

"I'm falling in love with you," Willis blurted. It was a lie, he was already head over heels for her.

She grinned. "That's good, because I'm halfway there myself."

Willis hadn't taken his hands from her face, and now he tilted her head up and kissed her lips gently. Then he tugged her against him and sighed in relief when her head came to rest on his shoulder.

"That was too close," he whispered into her hair.

"Yeah. I think I'm done with any kind of dangerous situations from here on out."

She *was* done. He'd make sure of it. He'd make it more than clear to his CIs that he wasn't a happy man. That Zero had gotten way too close to what belonged to Willis. It would most likely piss off the CIs that the man had managed to hide from their networks as well. Maylah would be the most protected woman in the DC area. Of that he had no doubt.

The sound of a car coming down the road made Willis lift his head. Maylah also turned with a sharp inhale.

"It's okay. It's Bull," he soothed.

The nondescript, dime-a-dozen navy blue four-door sedan passed the Volvo and pulled over in front of it. Bull got out, glanced at the ground, then continued to where Willis was standing with Maylah.

"Willis," he said with a lift of his head.

"Bull," Willis returned with a similar gesture.

"Hi!" Maylah chirped. "It's good to meet you. I understand you've worked with Greg for a while now? Thank you for your service. To him and to our country. And thank your wife too. I'm sure she misses you when you're gone on those jobs you do for Willis."

Bull's lips twitched upward. "Yeah. She does." He turned to Willis. "You good?"

Willis nodded.

Bull turned to Maylah again. "And you? He didn't hurt you?"

"No. Greg made sure of it."

"I bet he did," he said. "You ever need anyone to talk to, my wife, Skylar, would be happy to chat. She had a hard time dealing when she first learned what I did for Willis, but she came to terms with it."

"Oh, that's super nice. But I'm okay."

"Your man killed someone today," he pressed.

"Bull," Willis warned in a pissed-off tone.

Maylah straightened and met Bull's gaze head on. "Yes, I realize that. I was there. I didn't see it, but I heard it. It took like five seconds for Greg to not only disarm that jerk, but to make certain he could never rape me with a knife, as he'd threatened. So I'm not upset or weirded out or anything. Do I want him going out every night and taking down nefarious bad guys? No. But I understand more than some people how precious life is, and it's not like Greg is murdering people willy-nilly."

"Willy-nilly?" Bull asked with a small grin.

"You know what I mean," Maylah said with a wave of her hand.

Bull got serious. "I do. You should know, Willis is one of the best men I've ever met. For a Fed, he's pretty all right."

Willis rolled his eyes, but deep down was flattered. Being called "pretty all right" by this man was a compliment indeed.

Bull held his hand out to Willis and the two men shook.

"I'll get out of your hair so you can get back to whatever it was you had planned," Bull said.

"We're going to look at a five-year-old Great Dane who was chained up for his entire life and is scared to death of people," Maylah volunteered. "We want to foster him, but I've never had a giant breed like that before, so I have lots of questions about whether we'll be the best people to help him. Oh, and we have to see how Princess deals with other dogs in her space. Especially one who outweighs her by more than a hundred pounds."

"Princess?" Bull asked with a more natural smile.

"Yup. Greg adopted her. She's part Yorkshire terrier, Maltese, and beagle. She's small and fits in the crook of Greg's arm. Although with how Greg spoils her, I'm sure she won't be small for too much longer."

"Right." Bull shook his head. "Never thought I'd see the day. Happy for you, Willis. I'll be in touch if I have any issues, but don't expect I will."

Willis nodded at him, and when he stepped away to head back to the front of the Volvo, he turned Maylah so her back was to the car. He didn't want her to see Zero ever again.

"He seemed nice," Maylah told him.

"He is. Maybe we'll take a road trip to Indianapolis so you can meet his wife and the other guys who run Silverstone Towing."

"Really? You don't mind me meeting men who... you know...you employ?"

"Not these men, no. They'll take your safety just as serious as they do that of their own families."

"Then, yay, I'd love that."

Willis heard Bull's trunk close, and he took a deep breath. "I need to call the dealership."

"Will they be mad?" Maylah asked, turning to look down at the flat back tires.

"No."

She frowned up at him. "You sound so sure. *I'd* be mad if a car I'd loaned out for someone to test drive came back with two flat tires. With bullet holes in them at that."

"We're only about a quarter mile or so from Roberta's house, right?" Willis asked.

"Yeah, why?"

"Feel like a walk? It's a nice day. And I admit, I could use some time to try to reduce the amount of adrenaline still coursing through my bloodstream."

Just like that, concern shone in Maylah's gaze. "Are you all right?"

"Yeah. You okay with a little walk?"

"Sure. But how's that going to fix the car?"

"Trust me."

Maylah snorted. "Right. Okay. Let's go. I want to meet Oscar."

Willis gave Bull another chin lift after he did an impressive u-turn in the road and drove slowly past them. Maylah waved and smiled at him, making both men grin at her enthusiastic goodbye.

He eyed the ground where Zero had fallen and saw that Bull had done his best to cover up the large blood pool with dirt. Time and weather would take care of the rest of the evidence. He didn't miss how Maylah kept her eyes straight ahead as they passed the front of the SUV, then she began talking about Oscar and what she'd learned about Great Danes and their breed quirks.

She quieted long enough for him to call one of his connections to have him come out and change the tires on the SUV, and instruct him to bring it to the rescue group.

When she began chattering again, Willis was concerned that she was trying to hide any negative reaction to what had just happened, but as she continued, he realized that she seemed...lighter. That she was relieved to be out from under Zero's threats.

It was hard to believe she was truly all right with what he'd done, who he was, but the proof was in front of his face. It was one more sign that she was made for him. It might've taken almost five decades to find her, and a lot of heartache on both their parts, but today was the first day of the rest of their lives, and Willis vowed to make every day better than the last.

CHAPTER THIRTEEN

MAYLAH STOOD on the back deck and watched her husband play with the eight dogs in their backyard. It had been six years since she'd met Greg, and every day with him was a blessing.

They'd both sold their brownstones and pooled their money to buy the house they now lived in. It was a ranch, so there were no steps any of their wounded or skittish foster animals had to attempt to traverse, but the best thing was the huge yard. It was double fenced, the smaller area near the house was for when they first brought a foster home. The last thing they wanted was any of the dogs to run into the surrounding trees and hide out.

So they acclimated the new dogs they brought in until they weren't so skittish and scared anymore, then let everyone out to play in the larger yard.

Princess was the queen of the pack, and turned out to be better at putting new dogs at ease than they could've imagined. She took control, making sure everyone behaved, and she reveled in her role as alpha. Even at just ten pounds, her personality was large enough to keep everyone in line.

Maylah couldn't count the number of dogs, cats—and even the occasional goat—they'd fostered. Greg got attached to each and every one of them, and if he could, he would've kept them all. But Maylah constantly reminded him that if they adopted all of the animals, they wouldn't have room to help any others.

The animals were just as good for Greg as he was for them. He still worked a lot, but most of that time was from his home office. He only went into the city when necessary, and Maylah loved having him around.

Her love for him had only grown since their whirlwind courtship. She loved watching him work with Princess in his lap, a dog or two snoozing in one of the many dog beds in his office, and hearing him be all badass while talking to one of his CIs or dealing with some other intense situation.

The longer they were together, the more Maylah realized how many people her husband had truly saved. He wasn't on the front line, but without his research and the information he passed on to the men and women who worked for him, literally hundreds of people wouldn't have been rescued.

He was incredibly humble about it. Didn't like to be thanked. He always shrugged and said it was just part of his job. But Maylah saw the truth. He was an honest-to-God superhero. The people he arranged to be rescued might never know who to thank for their freedom, but Maylah knew.

"They're all a little hyper today," Greg said with a smile as he wandered up onto the deck toward her.

"Whose fault is that?" she asked wryly. She'd seen him get the pack all riled up.

He grinned. "A tired dog is a good dog," he quipped. "And I've got plans tonight that don't include letting Barry outside a thousand times just to have him *not* pee, and yelling at Camile to stop licking her sister's eyeballs."

Maylah giggled. Their current pack was a handful for sure. But she wouldn't have them any other way. "Plans? Oh, like working?"

"Nope," Greg said as he pulled her into his embrace.

"Plans like making another batch of dog food for the ones allergic to the commercial stuff?" she asked with a smile.

"Nope." Greg's head dropped and he nuzzled the sensitive skin of her neck.

"Oh, you must be tired and want to get some extra sleep."

"Yup. I want to go to bed early for sure," he drawled as one hand slipped beneath the elastic of her pants and gripped one of her ass cheeks.

Maylah smiled up at him. "I love you," she sighed.

"It's a good thing, since I love you too," Greg told her. He leaned down to kiss her but just then, Harry, Maisy, and Princess began to frantically bark.

They both turned their heads and saw Spot, their newest foster, had gotten his head stuck inside a log while on a walk one day.

Greg sighed, then said, "I'll go." He kissed her hard and fast and turned toward the stairs. Then he stopped and jogged back to where Maylah was standing. He took her face in his hands and kissed her deeply. They were both breathing hard by the time he pulled back.

"I'll never get enough of you. I'm the luckiest bastard in the world." He ran a finger down her nose and turned back to the stairs.

He yelled at the dogs as he rushed to rescue poor Spot. While he was bent over, Harry, the overweight lab mix they were fostering—trying to help him lose weight before being adopted—head butted Greg, making him fall to the ground laughing. Immediately, the pack thought this was a fun new game and everyone joined in, trying to lick and jump on their favorite human. Good thing Greg didn't wear his suits much anymore, now more at home in the jeans and T-shirts he typically put on every morning.

Maylah brought a hand up to her tingling mouth and smiled. Trusting Greg was the best thing she'd ever done in her life. It had brought her here. She was happier than she could ever remember being. Spending the rest of her life with him was a gift, one she never took for granted.

Turning slightly, she could see inside their large living area. On one wall was a picture of Elle and Molly, and one of Ted.

They never forget their first loves, and in a lot of ways, Maylah thought their common experience of losing a spouse was what drew them together so quickly.

"Thanks for watching over us," she whispered to all three of their lost loved ones. Then she closed her eyes and smiled. She was a lucky woman. Had an amazing life. She wouldn't trade anything about her past, because it had brought her to this moment.

Opening her eyes, she saw Greg looking up at her. "You good?" he asked.

Maylah smiled and nodded as she blew him a kiss. Tonight she'd show him exactly how good she was...as long as he was by her side. For now, she had dog food to make and laundry to do. Some might think her life was boring, but she'd take boring over excitement and danger every day of the week. She'd had enough of that to last her a lifetime.

———

Willis lay still, his arm around his wife, and smiled up at the ceiling. She'd fallen asleep almost immediately after she'd rolled into his arms after three very intense orgasms. He'd been almost insatiable, needing Maylah to know how much he loved her.

He did his best to make sure he showed her without words all the time, but tonight he'd been more than happy to show her physically. He enjoyed everything about making love with Maylah...especially how much she adored it when he went down on her.

He'd tired her out, but for some reason, he felt buzzed. Something drew him toward the large window near the bed. Willis slipped out from under Maylah, smiling at how she grumbled in her sleep. He leaned over, kissed her forehead, and promised to be back soon.

Then he walked naked as the day he was born over to the window, pulled back the curtain to look outside.

Just as he looked up at the dark night sky, a shooting star flew overhead. It was brighter than any he'd seen before, and it seemed as if the tail was twice as long as usual.

Willis smiled. "Hey, Elle. Hey, Molly. I hope you're okay wherever you are," he whispered. "I'm good. Really good. I miss you guys more than you'll know, but thank you for teaching me to live life to the fullest. I love her, so much, but that doesn't mean I didn't love you too. Thank you for being such an amazing wife, Elle, when I wasn't always the best husband."

An arm wrapped around him from behind, and Willis smiled as he turned into Maylah's embrace. She was also naked, and feeling her curves against his hard body felt amazing. "Why aren't you asleep?" he asked her.

"Couldn't sleep without you," she mumbled as she burrowed into him. Willis kissed the top of her head, and she looked up. "Are you okay?"

"Yeah."

"Good. Come back to bed," she cajoled.

He nodded and let her pull him to their bed. She climbed in and he scooted in after her. She immediately hitched a leg over his thighs and put her arm around his chest. He pulled her into him and felt her warm breath deepen as she eased back into sleep.

Closing his eyes, Willis sent a silent prayer of thanks to Elle, Molly, and even Ted, before falling into a deep, peaceful sleep of his own...the woman he loved in his arms.

* * *

If you haven't read the Silverstone series, you can start with *Trusting Skylar*, where Willis was first introduced!

Thank you for picking up this hodge-podge of stories, I love writing these and if you haven't met Baker, Tex, or any of the other characters, I encourage you to look up their stories!

Finding Jodelle (SEAL Team Hawaii series)
Protecting Melody (SEAL of Protection series)
Rescuing Annie (Delta Force Heroes series)
Marrying Emily (everyone shows up in this one!)

And of course NEXT up is *Deserving Henley*, the next book in my Refuge series! You met Henley in book one (the psychologist for The Refuge), and of course there's some nastiness that is lurking in the background!

*

Want to talk to other Susan Stoker fans? Join my reader group, Susan Stoker's Stalkers, on Facebook!

Don't miss a new release or a sale! Sign up for my newsletter on my website contact page:
https://www.stokeraces.com/contact-1.html

Also by Susan Stoker

Stand Alone:

A Moment in Time- A Collection of Short Stories
Another Moment in Time- A Collection of Short Stories
A Third Moment in Time- A Collection of Short Stories

SEAL Team Hawaii Series

Finding Elodie
Finding Lexie
Finding Kenna
Finding Monica
Finding Carly
Finding Ashlyn (Feb 2023)
Finding Jodelle (July 2023)

Eagle Point Search & Rescue

Searching for Lilly
Searching for Elsie
Searching for Bristol
Searching for Caryn (April 2023)
Searching for Finley (Sept 2023)
Searching for Heather (TBA)
Searching for Khloe (TBA)

The Refuge Series

Deserving Alaska
Deserving Henley (Jan 2023)
Deserving Reese (May 2023)
Deserving Cora (Nov 2023)
Deserving Lara (TBA)
Deserving Maisy (TBA)
Deserving Ryleigh (TBA)

Game of Chance Series
The Protector (Mar 2023)
The Royal (Aug 2023)
The Hero (TBA)
The Lumberjack (TBA)

SEAL of Protection Series
Protecting Caroline
Protecting Alabama
Protecting Fiona
Marrying Caroline (novella)
Protecting Summer
Protecting Cheyenne
Protecting Jessyka
Protecting Julie (novella)
Protecting Melody
Protecting the Future
Protecting Kiera (novella)
Protecting Alabama's Kids (novella)

Protecting Dakota

SEAL of Protection: Legacy Series

Securing Caite

Securing Brenae (novella)

Securing Sidney

Securing Piper

Securing Zoey

Securing Avery

Securing Kalee

Securing Jane

Delta Force Heroes Series

Rescuing Rayne

Rescuing Aimee (novella)

Rescuing Emily

Rescuing Harley

Marrying Emily (novella)

Rescuing Kassie

Rescuing Bryn

Rescuing Casey

Rescuing Sadie (novella)

Rescuing Wendy

Rescuing Mary

Rescuing Macie (novella)

Rescuing Annie

Delta Team Two Series

Shielding Gillian

Shielding Kinley

Shielding Aspen

Shielding Jayme (novella)

Shielding Riley

Shielding Devyn

Shielding Ember

Shielding Sierra

Badge of Honor: Texas Heroes Series

Justice for Mackenzie

Justice for Mickie

Justice for Corrie

Justice for Laine (novella)

Shelter for Elizabeth

Justice for Boone

Shelter for Adeline

Shelter for Sophie

Justice for Erin

Justice for Milena

Shelter for Blythe

Justice for Hope

Shelter for Quinn

Shelter for Koren

Shelter for Penelope

Ace Security Series

Claiming Grace
Claiming Alexis
Claiming Bailey
Claiming Felicity
Claiming Sarah

Mountain Mercenaries Series

Defending Allye
Defending Chloe
Defending Morgan
Defending Harlow
Defending Everly
Defending Zara
Defending Raven

Silverstone Series

Trusting Skylar
Trusting Taylor
Trusting Molly
Trusting Cassidy

Stand Alone

Falling for the Delta
The Guardian Mist
Nature's Rift
A Princess for Cale

Lambert's Lady

Special Operations Fan Fiction

http://www.AcesPress.com

Beyond Reality Series

Outback Hearts

Flaming Hearts

Frozen Hearts

Writing as Annie George:

Stepbrother Virgin (erotic novella)

ABOUT THE AUTHOR

New York Times, *USA Today,* and *Wall Street Journal* Bestselling Author Susan Stoker has a heart as big as the state of Texas where she lives, but this all American girl has also spent the last fourteen years living in Missouri, California, Colorado, and Indiana. She's married to a retired Army man who now gets to follow *her* around the country.

She debuted her first series in 2014 and quickly followed that up with the SEAL of Protection Series, which solidified her love of writing and creating stories readers can get lost in.

If you enjoyed this book, or any book, please consider leaving a review. It's appreciated by authors more than you'll know.

www.stokeraces.com
susan@stokeraces.com

facebook.com/authorsusanstoker

twitter.com/Susan_Stoker

instagram.com/authorsusanstoker

goodreads.com/SusanStoker

bookbub.com/authors/susan-stoker

amazon.com/author/susanstoker

Made in the USA
Middletown, DE
12 December 2022

18200197R00195